"Bolaño wrote that Rey Rosa 'is the most rigorous writer of my generation, the most transparent, the one who knows best how to weave his stories, and the most luminous of all.' Rigorous and luminous, spare and sensual, terse and hilarious, horrifying yet with a poetic, supernatural and metaphysical imagination, his writing—like that found in the novella *The African Shore*—throws open windows in your mind as you read."

—Francisco Goldman, *BOMB*

"Elegantly written, *The African Shore* conveys much information about cultures, past and present, along with the people who straddle the worlds of Europe and Africa . . . Stunning in the simplicity and clarity of its style, this novel says a great deal in very few words, and the ending is perfect."

—*Seeing the World Through Books*

"Rodrigo Rey Rosa is a Guatemalan novelist whose short, minimalist prose demands being sifted through to uncover layers and interwoven strands that make the reading of *The African Shore* a rich and intense experience."

—*New York Journal of Books*

FOR *THE GOOD CRIPPLE*, TRANSLATED BY ESTHER ALLEN

FOR *SEVERINA*,
TRANSLATED BY CHRIS ANDREWS

"Rey Rosa's book is both precious and precise. Its intense dreams, aphorisms, and literary lists are best read in one sitting. The author keeps readers on tenterhooks as issues of identity and desire ebb and flow along with a suspenseful episode involving the burying of a body. The fable here is a tale of love and forgiveness, which also includes the thievery of a book from Jorge Luis Borges's library. And while it would be impertinent to steal a copy, it is hard not to be tempted to grab a copy of this slim, terrific book."

—*Publishers Weekly*

"*Severina* is a satisfying, nicely crafted, and entertaining small tale of bookish obsessions, recommended to all who like a bit of clever literary fun."

—*Complete Review*

"*Severina* is a nuanced but passionate homage to the act of reading, to a life lived, as the narrator finally puts it, 'exclusively for and by books.'"

—*Zyzzyva*

FOR *DUST ON HER TONGUE*, TRANSLATED BY PAUL BOWLES

CHAOS,

A FABLE

OTHER TITLES BY
RODRIGO REY ROSA

CHAOS,

A FABLE

RODRIGO REY ROSA

Translated by Jeffrey Gray

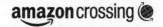

Text copyright © 2016 by Rodrigo Rey Rosa
Translation copyright © 2019 by Jeffrey Gray
All rights reserved.

Previously published as *Fábula asiática* by Alfaguara in Spain in 2016. Translated from Spanish by Jeffrey Gray. First published in English by AmazonCrossing in 2019.

Excerpt from "El aleph" by Jorge Luis Borges. Copyright © 1995 Maria Kodama, used by permission of The Wylie Agency LLC.

Published by AmazonCrossing, Seattle

www.apub.com

Amazon, the Amazon logo, and AmazonCrossing are trademarks of Amazon.com, Inc., or its affiliates.

ISBN-13: 9781542090353 (hardcover)
ISBN-10: 1542090350 (hardcover)
ISBN-13: 9781542090506 (paperback)
ISBN-10: 1542090504 (paperback)

Cover design by David Drummond

Printed in the United States of America

First edition

*For Xenia, who journeyed with me
most of the way.
For Pía, who had to remain home.*

I saw yet another wonder in the royal palace. It was a large mirror hung over a rather deep well. From down inside the well, you could hear everything men and women said on the planet, and, raising your eyes, you could see all the cities and all the towns, as if you were there among them.

—Lucian of Samosata, *True History*, Book One

PART ONE

On his last Sunday in Tangier, after giving a talk on the contemporary Mexican novel at the book fair, he visited Souani, a neighborhood in the lower part of Harun er-Rashid. He was looking for an old Moroccan friend of his whom he hadn't seen in almost thirty years, an artist and storyteller who claimed not to know his date of birth—though it was sometime around 1940.

A few days earlier, while stopping over in Paris, a Majorcan artist he'd just befriended had told him, "You've got to visit Mohammed. How long has it been? It's a pity, really. If you see him, give him my best."

The house stood on a small, steep street—Number Eleven of the new, labyrinthine medina—one among many three- or four-story houses painted white and blue and, lately, here and there, Marrakech red.

"It's been a long time, my friend, don't you think?"

Mohammed Zhrouni raised his hand to his lips, took the other man's hand, then touched his heart.

"Twenty years."

"A little more."

"Twenty-six, actually."

"Time doesn't exist anymore," said Mohammed. "The world has gone mad."

In the living room, on the second floor, they walked across a row of gaudy synthetic carpets. Mohammed offered him a seat on one of his m'tarbas, *the upholstered benches that lined the walls, and then, slowly and deliberately, sat down on the other side of the circular table in the middle of the room. He took off his slippers to stretch out on his own* m'tarba. *He sighed contentedly.*

"Hamdul-lah."

Rahma, Mohammed's second wife (his first had died years before) came in to serve tea. She still looked young, her skin pale and very freckled, her eyes large and furtive, her hair reddish in the style of people from the Rif.

They talked awhile of their families, as Moroccan etiquette requires: everything was fine, although Mohammed was quite poor and, in his old age, had been visited by a series of illnesses.

Fátima, Mohammed's oldest daughter, had gone with her husband to live in Almería, he said, from where she occasionally sent a little money.

His second son, Driss, lived in Tangier. "He's a bad egg," said Mohammed, laughing. "We never see him. He's a mechanic. He has a garage on the road to Achakar."

They sat quietly for a while, savoring the very sweet mint tea that Rahma had made. Mohammed said he no longer drank coffee, and also that he'd given up kif, Hamdul-lah.

"Remember John?"

The Mexican nodded. How could he not remember him?

John Field, the American artist and critic who'd spent the last half of his life in Tangier, had been a friend and mentor to both men. Over the years, he'd given Mohammed paper and Chinese ink, then canvas and paint, so that he could develop his talents. From time to time, he'd also gotten him out of financial difficulties, as a son or a close relative might do. And he'd provided the Mexican with contacts in the publishing world, helping him become a writer and translator.

"Well. Thanks to him, my son Abdelkrim is in trouble."

"Trouble?"

Mohammed stroked his jaw, covered with a few days' worth of gray stubble. The other man listened.

Abdelkrim, son of Rahma and Mohammed, not even twenty years old and highly intelligent, had gone to live in the United States.

"I'm going to ask you a favor, my friend."

"Yes, Mohammed."

Mohammed closed and opened his eyes, smiling. "Don't worry, it's not about money."

He stood up and crossed the small living room to a white chest of drawers with gold fittings. He pulled open a drawer and took

5

out a black plastic bag. While his guest watched him, he dumped the contents—some audio cassettes and a tiny memory card—onto the round tabletop between the m'tarbas.

"*I don't have any friends who know how to write,*" Mohammed said, staring at the cassettes. "*What am I?* Ualó. *Nothing. That's all right—I don't want to be anything! But when you have time, my friend, listen to what I say here.*" *He looked at him, then back at the cassettes.* "*You can turn these into books, if you want. You can write this.*"

"*Is it the story of Abdelkrim?*"

"*Yes. But also something more—much more!*"

"*Of course,*" *said the other. He asked what was on the memory card.*

"*I don't even know what that is, honestly. Abdelkrim sent it to Driss, and Driss brought it to me. I know nothing about such things.*"

The visitor took the card between two fingers, turned it over, and put it back on the table.

"*Can you see what's on there?*" *asked Mohammed.*

"*It could be photos,*" *he said.* "*Who knows? You don't have a computer?*"

"*No, no,*" *Mohammed laughed.* "*I've never touched one.*"

He kept looking at the cassettes and the memory card. Mohammed then carefully put them back in the plastic bag and handed it to his guest.

"Baraka lah u fik, *Mohammed*. Shukran b'sef."

He felt grateful, most of all, for the trust Mohammed was showing him.

"La shukran. Al-lah wa shib."

In Casabarata, a large flea market in Tangier, things went on as they had for thirty years. Vendors of all ages hawked their wares, reveling in a privilege afforded them by tradition: unmeasured time. Heaped among the rows of stalls, under laminate or cane awnings, the products of the new century—smartphones and LED lamps; multibladed vegetable choppers; fiberglass sinks and toilets, transparent or colored— lived alongside objects both timeless and of the past: typewriters, giant cigarette lighters, salt and pepper shakers, shoes and belts, mirrors and picture frames, suitcases and backpacks, vases . . . Would-be shoppers fingered the merchandise idly, with no apparent interest. It didn't take long to find a Sony double-cassette player in good condition. He picked it out of a twisted tower of tape decks. He asked the vendor if he could test it with an old cassette of Oum Kalsoum. It played smoothly.

The cassette player on his shoulder, he went out into the street swarming with people, not unusual for that time of day. Standing a few steps from a mosque under construction, he hailed a taxi to take him back to the hotel. The first thing he did once he got to his room was to test the cassette player again. After enjoying a light supper and a coffee on the corner, he returned to his room. He put the numbered tapes in order and lay down on the bed with the player, ready to listen.

7

The Future of Abdelkrim

I

The cassette was worn out and scratchy, but Mohammed's voice came through clearly enough:

After she gave birth to Abdelkrim, Rahma became very ill. To bring a child into the world requires money, and we had very little at the time. I went to visit John in Monteviejo, by the Sidi Mesmudi road.

Villa Balbina, a large two-story house, was surrounded by a garden and a little grove that looked out on the sea. I drew back the latch of the old metal gate, and two dogs—one white, one black—came running up the road, barking alarm. They knew me, but they didn't like me—I was a Riffi, and Nazarene dogs were wary of us.

A clump of tall reeds grew beside the gate. I cut a stick and pushed the gate, which squeaked open. The dogs were now a few feet away, barking and showing their teeth, but just lifting the stick over my head was enough to send them running.

From the stone terrace at the foot of John's room, I shouted up a good morning. John appeared on the balcony, knotting the belt of his silk bathrobe. He raised his hand, and in a voice of mock solemnity said, *"Salaam aleikum."*

He was an atheist dog, but I liked him.

"Aleikum salaam."

"Come in," he told me. "The door's open. I'll be right down."

His Spanish was almost perfect. It was easy to forget he was American.

I entered the big room with the fireplace, which was in use all year round except in July and August. Pines, cypresses, and eucalyptus trees surrounded John's house, so he was never lacking firewood. I sat down on a *m'tarba* under some colored tapestries and leaned back to wait for him. He didn't take long to come down.

"Hello, Mohammed."

"Hello, John."

He sat down on an old armchair, near the fire.

"I've asked Leila to bring us some tea," he said. "Or would you prefer something else?"

"Tea is fine."

"Everything all right?"

"Everything's fine."

"And Rahma?"

"She's fine. The baby was born five days ago."

"Hamdul-lah."

"Hamdul-lah."

We sat for a moment in silence. John looked out the window at some motionless clouds in the intensely blue sky. People called him the cloud painter. Maybe, as we sat there, he was thinking of his wife. She'd suffered a great deal, and he could do nothing to alleviate her pain. She'd also been an admirer of clouds. "The Moroccan sky is the bluest of all skies," she used to say. "And its clouds are the loveliest."

"We have to do the *aqeeqah*," I told him.

"Aqeeqah?"

"You know very well what it is, John."

In order to give a child his name, you must sacrifice two sheep—one, if it's a girl. I used to have a little piece of land the size of a fingernail but big enough to have chickens, a burro, some goats, and a couple of lambs.

"It's all very costly, John, but it has to be done."

"What's costly?"

"Buying a good sheep. Even a month's earnings aren't enough."

"I believe it."

"Can you help me, John?"

He looked unhappy.

"Of course," he said.

The next day we killed a goat kid in Mreier where my land was, and we listened to *jilala* music. A goat is just as good as

13

the lambs, and it costs less. When you're poor, this is permitted. The imam came and said a few words, and we gave my son the name Abdelkrim. John didn't come to the party, but when I went to visit him a few days later, he asked about the boy.

"It's a good name, Abdelkrim," he said, smoking a kif cigarette and following the winding smoke with his eyes. "Like the leader from the Rif, no?"

The next time I went to see him, I brought the boy with me.

"Is it done?" he asked me, after looking at the boy with interest.

"What?"

"The operation."

I laughed.

"Here we do it later," I told him. "It's important that the boy be aware of it." But I knew he didn't approve. "If you know what you're doing, it's perfect. We'll do it sometime in the next five years."

"Right, right," he said with displeasure, then changed the subject.

He had to get ready for friends who were coming to see him—gallery owners, collectors, admirers from Europe and America.

"There will be many guests. Can you help me?"

"How many guests?"

"About seventy."

"That's a good number, John. Seventy is no problem. I'll help you."

John bought a painting from me every year, more or less, and his friends, who came from far and wide to see him, especially during the summers, also became my buyers. You could say I lived on this income during that time—selling my paintings to the Nazarenes. May Allah, who forgives all sinners, forgive me.

II

Time does not exist. Five years passed, and the moment came to have Abdelkrim circumcised. Mouloud, the prophet's birthday, was approaching, so we decided to go with the boy to our *tchar* in the Rif. Before setting out, Rahma and the boy went to the hammam and came back home with their feet and hands patterned with henna. Rahma dressed him in new clothes: a white *casheb* and *saroueles*, a cap from Fez with a five-pointed gold star, and calfskin sandals.

I drove. I had the money John had given me to buy a bull and to pay the *tahar*.

In Sidi Ammar, we were greeted with shouts of merriment. At night the women gave money to Rahma, as was the custom—and still is, *Hamdul-lah*—and they served us heaping plates of couscous. The *moussem* is celebrated on a plain about an hour's walk from the *tchar*. A big black cloth tent is pitched over the saint's tomb, people come from other villages, and the cheer of women's voices can be heard throughout.

I took a seat at a makeshift café—set up among prickly pear trees covered with drying clothes—while Rahma went with the boy to buy sweets and a little meat from a newly sacrificed bull. I watched my borrowed money trickle away. Then she took the boy to a place forbidden to men, where the women paint their faces with root powders and kohl.

When the music began, the children lined up single file while the women shouted out *uyuyuys* and marked time with quick hand claps. Not long after, you could hear the boys' screams and weeping. The screams were so many and the cries so piercing that I had to get away. I walked up to a rocky mound at the far end of the esplanade and sat in the shade of a large boulder to smoke a few pipes of kif. I gave thanks to Allah, who had allowed me to save a few dirhams of the money John had given me for the bull. We had all shared the cost of the *tahar* between us, so that was a good thing.

I closed my eyes as I listened to the women's ululations and the boys' cries and the drums and claps. Before long, I heard a flutter of wings near my face. I opened my eyes. A huge crow had perched on a rock just beside me. It looked at me first with one eye, then with the other.

"*Salaam aleikum,*" I told it.

Then I heard, inside my head, "*Aleikum salaam.*"

We looked at each other awhile in silence. I refilled my pipe.

"Shni bghit?" I asked the crow, but it didn't answer. I drew on my pipe and blew out the smoke. "*Culshi m'sien?* Everything all right?"

"Culshi m'sien," I heard, again, in my head. "Everything is fine. Do you know who I am?"

"Yes," I said. "You're a friend."

The crow opened its beak and cawed.

"Your son, Abdelkrim, has a special"—or could it have said spatial?—"destiny in store for him. The whole world will know his name," the crow predicted from inside my head.

"Hamdul-lah!" I exclaimed.

"Listen, Mohammed," it continued. "Go get his foreskin while you still can. Put down your pipe and go. Now—before they bury it!"

A little confused (the kif?), I walked toward the tent over the saint's tomb and made my way as best I could to where Rahma and Abdelkrim were sitting. The *tahar* had just finished the circumcision. The boy was shrieking, and Rahma was consoling him. As is still the custom today, they had put the little ring of bleeding flesh in a small pot, full of earth from the saint's grave. If anyone saw me take it, they said nothing. It was as if, among the women, I had made myself invisible. The *tahar*, with his tweezers and his barber's razor, was concentrating on his next procedure.

I went back to the shady spot among the rocks where the crow was waiting. I opened my hand. The skin, covered with

19

dirt and blood, was almost black. The crow shook its head and stretched out its neck to its full length, its beak pointing upward. I knew what to do. I took the ring of skin—flesh of my flesh—carefully cleaned off the paste of earth and blood, and placed it around the bird's neck, which was so black it seemed blue. *What a beautiful necklace!* I thought. At that moment the crow, with a cry of triumph or of joy, took flight and disappeared beyond the mound of red rock.

I filled my pipe again.

III

The next cassette threatened to jam (a defective roller?). When it picked up again, Mohammed's voice began:

A lot happened in 1999. Abdelkrim fell terribly ill and nearly died. He suffered from high fevers in the morning and again at night. One morning his mother asked me to take him to the Spanish hospital. "If you'd gotten here any later," one of the doctors told me, "he'd have died. We'll have to admit him. But don't forget the money—can you get it?"

I left the boy with his mother at the hospital and went up to Monteviejo to see John. The white dog had died, and the black one didn't look like it had much time left. When it heard me, it got up, barked a little, then threw itself back on its straw mat next to the back door.

I found John sitting in the sun at the end of the terrace, in a wicker chair next to the big palm tree, his legs covered with a blanket. He was very thin.

"How are you, Mohammed. Everything all right?"

He seemed glad to see me. I hadn't visited him in months.

"Everything's fine, John. And you?"

He closed and opened his eyes. "I'm still alive. Would you like to sit down?"

He shouted something, and a servant I'd never seen before—tall and dark skinned—appeared.

I didn't like his face. From the Djebel, I thought. John asked him to bring me a seat.

"This is Abdelwahab," John said. "Mohammed is a friend."

"Welcome," said Abdelwahab.

I sat down, and the *djibli* went to the kitchen to make tea.

"How is Abdelkrim?" John asked.

At times, it was as if he read my thoughts.

I told him I'd taken the boy to the hospital early that morning. He understood.

We drank tea while the sun rose higher in the sky. The heat began to bear down on the terrace. Abdelwahab entered with a tray to collect the glasses and helped John out of his chair.

"I'll be back, Mohammed," John said. "You can wait here or, if you like, go into the living room."

"Ouakha."

John went into the house on the *djibli*'s arm, and I got up and took a walk around the terrace. Beyond the Bay of Tangier, you could see the Djebel Musa, clear and gray, like a resting camel.

Hamdul-lah, I thought.

John and the *djibli* came back a few minutes later. John took up his seat near the palm and waited for the other man to leave before handing me an envelope.

"To help cure Abdelkrim," he said. "I hope it's enough."

On my way back in the car, I opened the envelope. It was full of one-hundred-dirham bills.

In a matter of two weeks, the doctors had cured Abdelkrim—a virus, they said—and I didn't see John again until 2001, in September. John was from New York, but the last time he'd been there, the twin towers didn't even exist.

This time Abdelwahab took me into the living room, which was full of chimney smoke, and told me to wait there. A short time later, he announced that John would receive me in one of the rooms on the main floor, where he was confined to his bed.

"How are you, John?"

"As you can see. But sit down."

I sat at the foot of the bed.

"It's incredible," he said. "They've gone insane."

"You think there'll be a war?"

"There's already a war, isn't there?"

"A Muslim didn't do this," I told him. "That's impossible."

"Come again?"

"Believe me, John. The Jews did this."

He laughed, but I could see he didn't think it was funny.

"Right, a Jew named Mohammed Atta and another named . . ."

"Believe me, John. They're Jews."

"Well, they don't seem to be. Nor does their leader, what's his name, bin Laden."

"Al-lah hu a' lam," I answered. "Allah knows all."

In those days, many things ceased to be as they'd been. It was true that the world was going crazy; I didn't understand anything anymore. But I knew that the end, when Allah would settle all accounts, was drawing near.

Abdelkrim had turned eleven, and his mother insisted he should go to school. Not just to the *mçid*—the school attached to the mosque—which he already attended, but to another where he could learn a profession that would allow him to escape poverty. She wanted him to be an engineer, a lawyer, or a doctor— *"Something,"* she said. I was against it, but I gave my approval. John helped us enroll the boy in the American school, on Harun-er-Rashid.

Before he was sent to school, I used to take Abdelkrim fishing at Achakar, by the caves of Hercules, where the sea crashes against the rocks. We'd set out before dawn with poles and lines and whitings from the market. Sitting on the rocks, Abdelkrim would help me grind the tiny fish into a paste, which I'd mix with a little sand to make it heavy. Then we'd throw it into the water. The smell attracted the fish. The sea stirred up foamy eddies that murmured at our feet, while I told my son fantastic stories, and some true ones too. Then Abdelkrim started school, and all that came to an end.

I kept fishing when there was good weather, but I went alone, with my kif pipe. The world had gone mad, and I didn't care for it anymore. I no longer sought out my old friends. But Rahma was happy because the boy was healthy and his grades were very good.

"He's going to learn so much," she'd tell me. "When we're old, he'll take care of us better than anyone could, Mohammed."

I said nothing.

One morning while I was fishing in the usual spot, a very large crow landed by my side. It was a beautiful bird.

"Salaam aleikum," I said.

This must be the king of all crows, I thought to myself. It was huge. Its claws looked as if they were made of steel, its beak of crystal. But its plumage—how can I describe it? It was so black that when the light changed—the light trembles constantly when you're smoking kif—it threw off sheens of green and blue. It had golden eyes.

I asked it, "Are you the same bird I saw in Sidi Ammar?"

The bird spread its enormous wings.

"Listen!" I heard it say with perfect clarity—as I had heard it years before, inside my head. "Don't forget my words, because your fate and that of your entire city depends on what I'm about to tell you."

I responded by leaning forward.

"Your youngest son, Abdelkrim, was chosen by Allah to do great works. You, his father, must understand this. You must serve your son as if he were your lord. Watch him always, and see to it that his desires—even the very least of them—are fulfilled. Do as I tell you, but do it in secret. Not even the boy himself can know that the will of Allah, Lord of All Things, is that you and your family, but you especially, are to be his followers. The air and the clouds, the winds of the north and the south, the east and the west will be like brothers to him, as they are to me."

I heard a woman giggle behind me, then the voice of a man.

"Ashi, ashi, habibti."

I turned my head, but they were hidden among the boulders.

The crow took flight, and I watched it disappear between the rocks and the sea.

I reeled in my line and saw that the fish had carried off the bait. I threw the rest of the whitings into the sea and got ready to go back to the city. I thought of climbing up higher among the rocks and shaming the fornicators, but I let them be. May Allah judge them.

I headed back to Tangier by way of Mediuna, where the children sell pine nuts beside the road. I bought half a kilo. I wanted to make one of Abdelkrim's favorite desserts that afternoon.

IV

Slightly distorted on the tape, Mohammed's voice continued:

Time—our great friend, our great enemy—never stops, even though time doesn't really exist. That is the will of Allah.

One afternoon Rahma told me, "Mohammed, we have to go to the school. The principal wants to talk to us."

"Is something wrong?"

"I think they're going to give Abdelkrim an award."

"Ouakha," I said. "God is great."

I remembered what the crow had told me.

We were standing in the large office of the principal, Mr. Collins. On one wall hung a portrait of him in Moroccan attire—white djellaba, yellow slippers—posed against a background of blue sky and spongy clouds. It was one of John's paintings.

"Tswir," he said, looking at the portrait. "What do you think?"

Rahma was very happy, saying, *"Hamdu-li-lah, hamdu-li-lah."*

I was uncomfortable. He was principal of the school and, people said, a friend to King Hassan II and his son, the new sultan, but Mr. Collins was reputed to be a weekend drunk with a special fondness for boys. The stories of his binges and scandals were plentiful. He had a loud voice and every so often would burst into long guffaws. For this, he'd earned himself the nickname of *l-H'mar*, the donkey. He invited us to sit down. He looked at Rahma, then at me.

"How are you, Mohammed?" he asked in Spanish.

"Fine, Peter. And you?"

"How is our dear John?"

"I haven't seen him for some time."

"You should stop in and see him. I was with him on Sunday. He asked about Abdelkrim, and about you and Rahma as well. He thinks of you."

"Ouakha, I'll go and see him."

"Excellent."

He turned to look again, approvingly, at his portrait. Then he spoke.

"I've asked you here today to talk about Abdelkrim's future."

Rahma nodded her head eagerly.

"He's an extraordinary boy, as you must know. As parents of a boy like this, you have a special responsibility."

Rahma looked at me, her eyebrows raised.

"He has a unique intelligence, that's all there is to it," Mr. Collins continued. "As Rahma already knows, this year he has received the highest marks, not only in his class or his grade level, and not only of recent years, but the highest in the entire history of this school!"

He looked at me solemnly.

"Mohammed," he said. "I don't know what you think of such things, but we take them very seriously. I requested that Abdelkrim take a series of tests. About a month ago, I sent the results to a university in Massachusetts to get an expert opinion. Well, as it turns out, they're very excited to meet Abdelkrim over there."

He paused, as if waiting for a response. He looked at Rahma, then at me.

"Well," I said, "by all means, let them come meet him. *Marhababikum.* They are welcome."

"Yes, Mohammed. They have already come. They're here. And they have already spoken with Abdelkrim. They're even more impressed than they were before! They say they want to take him to America—not immediately, but soon, and with your permission—so he can continue his studies, special studies, very special, with other boys like him, in a special American school."

I shook my head. "Peter, thank you very much, but no."

Mr. Collins looked at Rahma, who nodded yes.

"Mohammed," said Mr. Collins, "I want you two to discuss this calmly before you say no. Would that be all right?"

"Ouakha," said Rahma.

"Fine," I said, and got up.

"Thank you, Mohammed." Mr. Collins stretched out his hand to give me a firm, emphatic handshake. I touched my chest. He added, "My congratulations to you. Your son is a genius, a gift from Allah."

"Báraca l-lah u fik," said Rahma. She kissed her own hand and held it out to Mr. Collins. *"Shukran b'sef."*

"La shukran, Al-lah wa shib," he said with a strong American accent.

We crossed the office. I looked back at the portrait John had painted of Mr. Collins, looking petulant in Moroccan dress, the sky and clouds behind him. *"Zamil,"* I thought.

"And Mohammed!" Mr. Collins shouted from his desk as Rahma and I were leaving. "You must go and see John sometime soon. I think he's not well."

"Ouakha," I said.

"Give him my regards."

"Ouakha."

Rahma didn't speak until we were in the car.

"Mohammed, we must think carefully about what we're going to do—not for us, not for me or you, but for Abdelkrim."

I nodded my head. *"Bismil-lah,"* I said, and started the car.

"In the name of God," Rahma repeated. "It is he who knows."

It was around this time that the Americans hanged Saddam Hussein, their old friend. That is how they are, and Saddam was wrong to trust them.

I talked with Rahma about what was happening in the world. I reminded her of the first Gulf War. "The Americans did it," I told her, "to deceive the public. What they wanted was oil, and to make people forget about President Clinton and the Lewinsky woman.

"They declared the other Gulf War," I went on, "because they wanted more oil and, by the way, to sack Iraqi treasures. They said Saddam had weapons to destroy the world, but they didn't find any, of course, because it was a lie," I said. "That's the way they are, Rahma, and so be it. But we should not believe them."

"You're right," she answered. But she insisted we had to think of Abdelkrim.

And Abdelkrim—I wondered—*what will* he *think?* I didn't want to ask him about it.

"Go and talk with John," Rahma said. "See what he thinks."

V

John sat in an armchair in his Moroccan-style living room on the first floor, surrounded by visitors. His legs were covered with a wool blanket, as was his custom lately, and his head was tilted backward. He didn't look sick to me. He made introductions: two old woman painters, one from Paris, the other from New York; a professor from Boston, Massachusetts; a German journalist; a young Mexican writer.

"Sit down, Mohammed," John said. I sat on the *m'tarba* near the Mexican.

The *djibli* came in, and I asked for coffee. I took out my kif pipe.

Everyone was speaking French and English. They directed their conversation almost exclusively to John. The Mexican, to my right, said nothing, his eyes moving from one speaker to the next. If he didn't understand what was being said, it seemed as though he were trying to capture their words with his gaze.

I offered him my pipe, and he accepted.

The woman from New York wanted to buy one of John's recent paintings, part of a series he had done in bed while he was recovering from pneumonia. They were violent panoramas, skies covered with storm clouds of the kind you see in the winter over the strait between the columns of Hercules—Djebel Musa on this side, Djebel Tarik in Spain.

The French woman wanted to show John some drawings she had been working on that week in the medina.

She was the one who mentioned Saddam. The other one said she hoped they'd catch Osama bin Laden someday.

John said to the Mexican, "I like the idea of this man escaping the Americans on horseback across the desert under the moonlight. It would make a good painting, wouldn't it?— if, say, Delacroix had painted it."

The Mexican agreed. "Or Rousseau?" he said, laughing.

The two women didn't find this funny. Why romanticize a terrorist? Was he not a big terrorist, bin Laden?

"Oh yes," John said. "We trained him, after all."

The painters changed the subject, telling John that they would come back the next day to visit him, a little earlier, so they could have him to themselves. Then, followed by the German, they said their goodbyes. The Boston professor, the Mexican—now very high—and I were the only ones left.

"How is Abdelkrim?" John asked me.

The professor fixed his gaze on me with his big round glasses. He was a thin man, his shoulders sloped with a small, barely visible hunch.

"Abdelkrim?" he asked, looking at John. "The same Abdelkrim?"

"The same," said John. "This is his father, Mohammed."

"Ah, *muy bien*," said the professor, who spoke Spanish.

"This man," said John, "has been telling me that your son is quite a marvel."

I looked at him sideways, clicked my tongue, and said, "What can I say, John? He's a little boy. Little boys are almost all marvelous."

"Well, yes," John said.

The Mexican choked back his laughter. I looked at him and laughed as well.

"No, no," the professor said. "This boy is unique. Let's not confuse things."

Without looking at the professor, I said to John, "Some people think they know more than others because they've read a lot of books or gone to school. But true knowledge isn't in books. It's here." I put my hand on my chest, over my heart. "Allah puts it there. Books are for those whose hearts are empty. Maybe their brains too. They've got to fill them up with something."

"Yes, you're filling them up with smoke," the professor muttered in English very quietly, but I understood.

"When this piece of carrion leaves," I said to John in Maghrebi, "we can talk."

"Ouakha," said John.

He called the *djibli* to light the fire in the fireplace. The professor stood up to say goodbye. The Mexican, completely *mkiyif* by now, did not react. After the professor left, John offered us more tea.

VI

Mohammed continued:

We were silent while Abdelwahab lit the fire. As usual, he used too many eucalyptus leaves, and the room filled with smoke. I opened a window across from the door so the smoke could circulate; in a short time the air in the room became breathable again, and the flames flickered happily in the fireplace.

The Mexican had drunk his cup of tea. I laughed at him and said, "That's how the *djebala* drink their tea."

"The *djebala*?"

"The people from the countryside. From the Djebel. Like that one," I said, looking in the direction of the kitchen, where Abdelwahab was working.

"The Riffians don't like the Djebel people," John explained to him, "and the *djebala* don't like the Riffians."

The Mexican blushed.

"Ah," he said, and looked into his empty cup.

"It's all right," I said. "But it's better to drink it slowly and to always have a little left in the cup to go with the kif."

John nodded.

"The great smokers say so," he told the Mexican.

"They call it *al deqqa*," I added. "Fairly hot and with plenty of sugar. It keeps the smoke from making you nauseated. If you don't have the tea, you might throw up. Or faint. Believe me."

"I can vouch for that," John said.

"That's good to know," the Mexican said. And a moment later he stood up, saying, "You two have important things to talk about. I should get going."

"No, my friend," I said. "You can stay—please."

The Mexican looked at John, who nodded his head.

"Thank you," the Mexican said, and sat down again. He leaned back on the *m'tarba*, listening.

A moment later, I said, "John, what do you think? Why are the Americans so interested in Abdelkrim?"

"Hmm," said John, looking straight in front of him. "*Manarf.* I don't know."

"John, you know very well."

"No, seriously. It seems your boy has an amazing head. That interests the Americans very much—no doubt about it."

"His head?"

"His brain."

I shook my head doubtfully, making a face. "It's strange, very strange," I said. "I was just like him as a kid. And his brothers, the ones with the other mother, were also very intelligent. But they didn't get very far. Abdelkrim is the smartest."

"The others didn't go to school," John said.

"School," I said. "That's where the problems start."

I looked at the Mexican, who nodded.

"Bokó Harám," he said, smiling. "It's true."

"It's true," I repeated. "John, remember that crow that talks to me sometimes?"

"Yes, I remember," John said.

And I told him again about the time the crow came to visit me among the rocks while I was fishing.

"Amazing," said John.

"Incredible," said the Mexican.

"So what do you think you'll do?"

"I don't know."

"Righto," said John.

"But if they want to take him to America," I said a moment later, "they're going to have to give us a lot of money."

"Money they do have," John said. "That's for sure."

VII

Time does not exist. Today we're here, and tomorrow, who knows? said Mohammed's voice on the final cassette.

I let the Americans take Abdelkrim off to Massachusetts. It wasn't just for the money. He wanted to go. He told me so, in the name of Allah.

Rahma talked to him often on Skype. He told us he had a Nazarene friend. Greek, I think. May Allah forgive us!

He completed his engineering degree and then went on to study electronics, and I don't know what else. By the end of the year, he had enrolled in aviation school. I didn't understand a thing about it, but Rahma explained it to me. If all goes well—Abdelkrim told her—he'd get his American citizenship and become an astronaut.

I didn't and I *don't* believe any of that. No more than I believe the Americans went to the moon—pure propaganda. Lies, nothing more.

John was getting weaker and weaker, and I began to visit him more often. It bothered me to see how the *djibli* was mistreating him and stealing from him.

"Hamdul-lah," John would say, as if he were a Muslim.

Near death, he kept on working, almost always in bed. He was still painting cloudscapes. The last one he painted showed a pale but very large sun, as if seen through a magnifying glass, the way it had looked on the afternoon he died, a week before the Americans brought down Osama bin Laden in Abbottabad.

Boujeloud

I

The shrill, piercing notes of a rhaita traveled over the night air and into the Mexican's room. He thought of Boujeloud, a syncretic incarnation of the god Pan and the Moroccan scapegoat. Once a year, this ancient spirit of fertility, covered with goat skins and armed with two branches of olive or oleander, went out into the streets with a retinue of hornpipes and drums to sow panic among women and children, until, all at once, they would turn against him and chase him out of town. *Mohammed's story could be the beginning of a book,* the Mexican said to himself. He'd enjoyed hearing himself included in it! But it was too late, and he was too tired now to see what was on the memory card. He set the tape player down on the floor next to the bed, put out the light, and covering his face with one arm, went to sleep.

• He woke up earlier than usual, thinking of Abdelkrim. He wondered how much fabrication there could be in a story like that. What was the point of it all? He ate breakfast quickly in the hotel restaurant so that he could return to his room, where, instead of writing in his diary as he usually did, he turned on his old laptop. He inserted the memory card, but the format was incompatible with his PC. He clicked cancel. Nothing happened. He took out the card, and the screen declared, "Error!"

Searching for a computer to read the memory card, he walked as far as the old Calle Velázquez—whose new Arabic name he didn't know—and went into a *téléboutique*.

The girl at the counter tried the card in one of the shop computers, but like him, she had to force it back out of the slot. "You need a Mac, sir," she said. "We don't have any here."

After a light lunch in a hotel garden on Avenida Istiqlal, he walked to the Zoco de los Bueyes, at the top of a hill overlooking the city. He spent some time walking around the neighborhood. The crickets, the dogs, the odd donkey, the cars and their horns; in the distance, an oil tanker crossing the strait; and the continual whistling of the *cherqi*—all of this was as it had been thirty years earlier. Finally, he walked down Calle Imam Kastalani and, with a curious mix of wistfulness and happiness, approached an old five-story building, where one of his oldest Tangier friends lived.

Before he knocked on the apartment door, which was on the top floor, and while he caught his breath (the elevator wasn't working), he heard voices inside. A man was shouting in Darija—it seemed he was on the phone—while a woman's voice was asking him to help her move furniture in the living room.

The person who opened the door was thick lipped, his beard several days long. His pointed, satyr-like ears protruded from under graying curls.

"Rubirosa!" the man exclaimed, holding out his arms to the Mexican. *"Marhababek! Dghol, dghol."*

"Ah, Boujeloud," he said, joking. "I heard the rhaita playing last night. Was that you? That's the sound that brought me here."

Boujeloud, master of the Moroccan rhaita and guimbri, was the leader of a band from a *tchar* to the south of Tangier, where many pre-Islamic customs survived. Legend had it that he'd recorded with the Rolling Stones. The American woman he'd married now worked as the band's honorary manager.

They embraced.

"Carrie, look who's here," said Boujeloud in English.

Carrie, a New York photographer, Tangerine by adoption, was still in pajamas and looked as if she'd just woken up. In the living room, she hugged their guest and kissed him on both cheeks. She invited him to sit and told Boujeloud to make some tea.

"It's been so long since you've visited, Rubirosa," Carrie began. She was the one who'd given him that nickname—after the notorious Porfirio Rubirosa—in response to the one he'd given her husband: Boujeloud. "How have you been? We heard you were in Tangier but didn't know if we'd get a chance to see you."

The Mexican began to sum up his life over the past ten years—he had last seen Carrie and the musicians in New York in 2011 at a concert they played in Central Park. He'd published five books since then. He couldn't complain, he said. He'd gotten married in 2012 and divorced in 2014. He'd been invited to the Tangier book fair, which was why he was here now. He told them about his meeting with Mohammed the day before and—in broad strokes—the incredible story of his son Abdelkrim.

Carrie and her husband exchanged a look.

"Mohammed and Boujeloud aren't friends," she said with a smile.

"He's a thief," said the Moroccan faun.

"I don't know," she explained. "They've had problems. You know, Rubirosa—the people from the Rif hate the people from the Djebel, and vice versa. But we've heard about Abdelkrim. They say he's a genius."

"A djinn?" Boujeloud asked, laughing loudly.

As he told them the boy's story, Carrie began to take pictures. At sixty, she still had the body and the energy of youth. She dashed from one side to the other with her camera in search of different angles.

"My laptop won't accept Mohammed's memory card," the Mexican said. "I still haven't been able to open it."

Carrie volunteered her Mac. Boujeloud inserted the card, and this time the files opened. There were three Word documents and a series of images, among them a skull and crossbones, which Boujeloud said he didn't like. The first document was written in Maghrebi with Arabic characters. It was a letter from Abdelkrim to his brother Driss—sent from Andover, Massachusetts, Boujeloud said. He began to translate aloud.

He stopped from time to time to exclaim in his rough English, "Incredible, Porfirio! What is this shit?"

He was sure it was all lies—about Abdelkrim's classes at the University of Massachusetts, about his training to be an astronaut, and about the Greek friend who was a millionaire—or perhaps a billionaire.

"You're crazy, you know?" he said in English.

He burst into laughter, then went back to reading the letters and emails, the contents of which—the Mexican was sure—Abdelkrim's parents (who were illiterate) could not have been aware.

"It's no problem, Rubirosa," said Carrie finally. "You're my brother, aren't you? Take the laptop. Use it. And return it when you've finished your work, which seems fantastic. Tomorrow or the next day would be fine. Anyway, we have another one. And everything important is in the cloud."

Boujeloud asked him if he needed a ride anywhere.

When their visitor declined the offer, Boujeloud explained that not long ago they'd purchased a Mercedes-Benz, barely used, in Spain. If he wanted, they'd let him drive it. He finally accepted, though insisting he'd rather not drive.

Boujeloud drove him in his Mercedes through the crowded streets of Tangier, filled with cars and people. At the entrance to Hotel Atlas, they hugged goodbye and kissed each other on both cheeks.

"B'slemah."
"B'slemah."

Aljamía

I

Yimma, Ba!

I hope, Mother and Father, under God's protection, you are happy to be on Earth. I miss you both very much. Were it not for the will of Allah, I would be with you!

They won't let us use Skype for now. For security, they say.

From my apartment, which is in a tall building, I can see the ocean. The moonlight plays on its surface, and I think of Ba, who told me fantastic and funny stories when he took me fishing on the rocks.

It's nighttime, and I'm ready to drop after a long day of study and exercises. We're studying the properties of the wind. Each layer of air is different, they say.

Only Allah knows all!

I miss you.

II

Yimma,

I now have to shave the fuzz on my cheeks!

The last time we spoke you asked me whether living here—where the will of Allah, the merciful, has brought me—doesn't make me feel lonely, whether I've been able to make friends.

Ba was worried, you said, that I might be making friends among the Nazarenes and Jews and other infidels. He's heard it's a sin to have these kinds of friends, although he's done the same himself—in fact, Ba has worked for the Nazarenes in Tangier almost all his life. I suppose what you've heard are the words of the imams of Souani and Emsallah, who, from what you tell me, are sages and saints.

Here, apart from studying everything about the great ball of the world and the other planets, I'm also allowed to study the Book. I devote at least an hour a day to reading it. The Koran is truly beautiful. Concerning friends, I found some verses (2:62) that perhaps you would like to hear, if someone would be so kind as to read them to you:

> *Those who believe, without a doubt, those*
> *who practice*
> *Judaism, or the astrology of the Sabians, or*
> *Christianity,*
> *Those who believe in God and who on the*
> *Last*
> *Day do good deeds, all of these need not*
> *Fear, for they will not be afflicted.*

Perhaps you can ask the imams to tell you, according to them, what these lines mean.

III

I have a new friend. He's the descendant of a prince from a time when Morocco did not yet exist and was populated by lions and savage tribes—or at least that's what he says. This prince was a mathematician and an astronomer and studied the sun and the stars, the moons and the planets. He was the first to divide the year into 365 days of 24 hours each (plus 5 hours, 46 minutes, and 24 seconds).

I'd tell you of another science we have to study to become pilots—and, if Allah so wishes, astronauts. It is the science that studies shadows—there are both dark and white shadows—as well as triangles, pyramids, and spheres. But I don't want to bore you!

Xeno is, first and foremost, a great friend. He tells me that when we get a vacation, he'd like to make a stop in Tangier—on the way to Athens, where he was born—to meet you and Ba. He asked me to teach him Arabic, and in a matter of days, he learned the numbers and the alphabet. Now we write each other in English using Arabic letters—a new kind of Aljamía—so that no one else can understand our messages. And for his part, he's teaching me Greek.

IV

Dear all,

I'm writing you today from a place far south of Massachusetts, called Merritt Island, in Florida. It's hot and very humid here, it can rain at any moment, and the air is full of insects. *Hamdul-lah!*

As I told Yimma a few days ago on Skype, I've been chosen, with about twenty other students, selected from thousands, to enter a special program at NASA. In a few months, once I have my American citizenship, we'll become real astronauts. (They might give me honorary citizenship for being an "alien of extraordinary ability." That's what they gave Albert Einstein and other "aliens"!)

Do you remember, Yimma, how Ba used to say that the story of man on the moon was a lie, mere propaganda by the Americans, who want to seem as powerful as God himself, so as to be admired above all humanity? Well, people who make such arguments are mistaken. Allah made us intelligent and bold and capable of great works because it pleases him to see his creatures understanding and conquering not only the ball of the world but the whole universe!

V

Today is a bad day, Driss.

I told you all that they were going to grant me US citizenship. Today I got a letter saying the request has been denied. Why? I'm too Muslim!

I'm not coming home yet. I will keep you informed.

I miss you.

PART TWO

PART TWO

Xenophon

Xenophon has notable defects: He is not thorough in his gathering of data. He is forgetful and marginalizes facts of primary importance. And he narrates events from his own perspective.

—Greekipedia (June 26, 2016, 11:00 a.m.)

I

Xeno jumped out of the old fishing boat onto the concrete pier on the island of Leros—the island of windmills and barren hills, the island of the asylum—where the rough sea mixed with the sky. As waves rocked the boat, he lifted out his father's heavy leather suitcase, in which they'd packed the medications purchased in the only two pharmacies on the neighboring island of Patmos. The captain shouted over the whooshing of the wind and the crashing of the waves, "At seven! *Stis epta! Epta!*" and with a turn of the rudder, the boat moved away from the dock.

A black male nurse (Red Cross and Red Crescent) waited on the dock. He invited Dr. Galanis and his son to climb into a little English jeep. Xeno took the back seat, leaning forward to hear his father's conversation with the nurse.

"How many?" asked Dr. Galanis.

"Thirty-four," the nurse said. "Yesterday there were almost a hundred. Meningitis. They're going crazy all at once."

"What kind of meningitis?"

The nurse shrugged his shoulders. "Epidemic," he said.

"They can't just keep coming like this."

"They're not coming because they want to," Xeno said.

"Something has to be done so that they won't want to come," replied the nurse.

"They're biological bombs," said his father, looking to his right at a number of orange spots vibrating in the distance. The nearest ones suddenly became a line of points of the same color and were then transformed into several dozen passengers in life jackets. "That's what they are."

These days there were fewer deranged patients in the hospital, the nurse explained. They'd all, with the exception of the terminal patients, been evacuated after the "scandals." He was referring to certain articles in the European press that had appeared some decades earlier, denouncing the deplorable state of the mental hospital on Leros, which the newspapers called "the island of the mad." Now the sick immigrants were being taken to ward 16—a kind of large, covered pool with a ceramic floor and very high walls.

"Do you know the hospital?" the nurse asked.

The doctor ignored the question. "Are they exposed to the sun?"

"There's a shady area. It's not an attractive place," the nurse added. "In the middle of the floor, the shit gets mixed in with the leftovers. There is hardly any bedding. And not a single

70

mattress. We have one plate for every five or six people, and one glass for every ten. At least there are fewer things to wash."

"How many doctors?"

"Today, just you. And there are no antibiotics, no painkillers, not even aspirin. Frankly, there's not much to do."

The old Italian prison, converted first into a mental hospital and now into a refugee asylum, stood in the middle of a valley full of willows. At the tall metal gate, a guard let them in almost without a glance.

"Masks?"

The nurse shrugged. He had one, he said, pulling a mask out of the pocket of his smock.

They crossed over the main patio under tall Italian arches. A number of elderly terminal patients were stretched out on the floor in the hopes of catching a few weak rays of sun. Dr. Galanis stopped at the entrance of ward 16. He took out a mask from his suitcase, handed it to Xeno, and, using a gauze bandage and a handkerchief, fashioned another for himself.

"Saliva is very dangerous," he said to Xeno. "Cover up your mouth and nose. And don't take it off till we've left."

"Of course."

They put on their masks.

In ward 16, they found refugees of all ages. Stretched out against the entire length of the walls, they kept very near to each other to stay warm. The smell of their bodies and their waste was like a subtle, greasy gas that penetrated the visitors'

71

nostrils, in spite of the masks. Xeno at one point had to stop himself from vomiting.

The doctor turned on a small flashlight. "The light is very irritating if you have meningitis," he said.

"Of course, Father."

In a corner under a high window with clouded panes, mothers and their babies sat together on the ground. The doctor put on rubber gloves and knelt beside a woman holding a two- or three-year-old girl in her arms. He opened the suitcase and took out a stethoscope. He frowned as he listened to the child's heartbeat and again as he felt her neck, armpits, and abdomen. The girl seemed not to notice anything. The doctor had her lie on her side on the floor, then drew up her knees in a fetal position, with her chin touching her thorax. He took a roll of sterile cotton out of the case, tore off a piece, and soaked it in alcohol to clean her back. He let the little ball of blackened cotton fall, and the nurse gave it a kick toward the middle of the floor. The doctor turned to Xeno and asked for a syringe. He had to take a sample of spinal fluid—a lumbar tap. They would make a culture. But first he needed to anesthetize her, he said.

In the beam of the flashlight, he saw that the girl's mother had both arms covered with reddish-black stains; they looked like hematomas caused by a beating.

He would have to amputate the infected limbs as soon as possible, the doctor said.

"We have saws. There's plenty of alcohol," said the nurse, "and sponges. But that's about it."

In addition to English, the nurse spoke Turkish and Syrian Arabic; he asked the children to sit up and remain seated with their backs against the walls. Dr. Galanis began to distribute medications, but they soon ran out. It was an act more merciful than therapeutic. Xeno helped to place pieces of cardboard under the jaws of the seated children, asking them to hold the cardboard there, applying pressure on the thorax. Those unable to do so were separated and led to one of the communal baths, where they would remain isolated from the rest.

The doctor took a little tube of alcohol gel out of his pocket. He disinfected his hands and had Xeno do the same.

II

It was in the library of the Byzantine monastery of Saint John the Theologian, on the island of Patmos, that one of the monks realized Xenophon Galanis had a prodigious mind. At seven years old, he could already read manuscripts in eleventh-century Greek. That summer, he began spending the first hours of each morning in monastic calm, examining volume after volume, while other children his age played on the beaches or sailed in their parents' boats and yachts. In the afternoon, when a cruise ship arrived at the small port of Scala, the happy, big-eyed, chubby-cheeked child offered his services as guide to those who came up to Khora to visit the holy cave. It was in this cave, around AD 95, that Saint John dictated his hallucinatory end-of-the-world vision. The cave lay not far from Xeno's parents' house, and the monks who ran it were his friends.

"I think the child wants to join our congregation," said the abbot one day to Xeno's mother, an art collector of English descent.

"You're mistaken, Father," she said with a mix of pride and humor. "He wants to be a saint!"

"That's what I meant" was the abbot's presumptuous response. He was a Greek from the nearby island of Kos—bearded, well-mannered, and corpulent.

At the age of nine, however, during a family dinner in the house in Khora, Xeno declared he was thinking of studying art history. His older sister, whom he worshipped, had done the same and was now a curator of Byzantine art at an important London museum.

His father objected.

"It's a wonderful occupation, my dear Xeno, and you must forgive my saying this, but there are more suitable things for a boy like you. You will understand later on."

Xeno did not contradict him. His mother and sister refrained from commenting. They were dining on the terrace of the little garden, which looked out over the southern part of the island. A small and very white solitary cloud rose in the light-purple sky of the east, opposite the sun, sinking in the Aegean.

"It seems they used to have an alarm system that was controlled by the monks," the boy said. "It connected the monasteries, which were also forts, to alert the communities to approaching enemies—Venetian or Barbary pirates or whoever. That's how they were able to prevent surprise attacks. The network reached from Constantinople to Jerusalem and Rome, including several islands of the Dodecanese, like Patmos and Leros. There were monasteries every fifty or seventy kilometers. And the oven in the monastery wasn't just used for baking bread." Xeno turned his gaze to the hilltop, toward the monastery, which rose above the island and, along with the Cave of the Apocalypse, stood as its powerful emblem.

"Also for scorching infidels?" his sister joked.

"For boiling olive oil to pour down the sluices," corrected their mother.

"Amounts to the same thing," their father said.

"They may have used it to make smoke signals," Xeno continued. "In one of the books at the library—copied by an eleventh-century scribe who was the eunuch of an Abbasid conqueror and later became a monk—you can see the first report of the Romans' defeat at Manzikert. No one had foreseen it. It was the monks who spread the news. In our monastery there are two chimneys in the rooms where they knead the dough. Between the chimneys a crucible is built into the base of the oven. The abbot thinks they used it to make pigment from zinc."

"That's all recorded in the book?" his sister asked.

"There's residue in the rock. They would have been able to make white smoke," Xeno said. "One of the monks would have kept watch, scanning a specific part of the horizon at a specific time. They probably used a kind of Morse code. Someone had to watch. Someone had to be there."

His sister laughed and then said, "Bravo! It seems obvious. When Constantinople fell, they say people in Rome knew immediately. Three hours—with the time difference? It must have been a very clear day in this part of the world! Do you know what they're still saying today in Rome?"

"The Catholics?" said their father with contempt.

"That the pope got the news in a vision," she continued. "A mystical vision. More likely he got it by optical telegraph—that's great, Xeno!"

"I don't doubt it," their father said, fondly stroking the head of his prodigy. "We'll have to keep it in mind for the day when there's no more internet."

By the age of twelve, Xeno's interests shifted to mathematics. He had stood out from an early age at Byron College in Athens. Then he was accepted at the Cambridge Faculty of Mathematics. He read with Griffiths ("No Consecutive Heads") and George ("Testing for the Independence of Three Events"). A year later he was admitted to the East Anglian Rocketry Society. "Thank God for our English grandfather," his sister commented when Xeno shared the news. Later, he traveled to Boston, where he entered MIT, taking courses in aerodynamics, astronomy, and astronautics.

III

It was during a round of talks on the future colonization of the Lagrangian points, at Singularity University in Silicon Valley, that Xeno met Abdelkrim. Even though the backgrounds of these two unusual minds could not have differed more, they agreed in many of their responses to the problems of manned space voyages. On the basis of these theoretical affinities, the two young men formed a close friendship. They had both been hired to work at the Ames Research Center in Mountain View, California, and thus they were able to spend time together and develop ideas over months of constant discussions. What good would all the knowledge that mankind might accumulate by natural or digital means do—they sometimes asked themselves, already in full mystical mode—if it didn't reduce human suffering at least slightly? And was the prolonging of human life justified in ethical terms when it seemed clear that mankind had entered a period of terminal disintegration and destruction? (The attacks on Brussels and Paris were not far off.) Could they not imagine for the human species a situation in which death by fire would be a welcome liberation from the inferno of life? Wasn't it possible, in fact, to make a case for universal euthanasia? Or were we condemned, out of loyalty, to hope for the continuation of the species, no matter the suffering? Thinking of something he'd read the night before by Paul Bowles, Xeno asked, "Wouldn't it be better to go back technologically to where humanity found itself in the Middle Ages—to begin again from there and take a less violent path?"

"I'd say much further back," the Moroccan replied. "Back to the Stone Age."

One afternoon, riding in Xeno's compact Range Rover on the way to Tassajara, they'd gotten farther than usual off the winding desert tracks and became disoriented. They had smoked some of the local cannabis (Purple Helmet) and from time to time broke into bouts of hysterics for no reason. A few days earlier, Xeno had suggested to Abdelkrim that he read *The Aeneid*, and now the Moroccan quoted the scene in which Aeneas gathered a group of young men for a test of prowess; a young warrior shot an arrow upward with such strength that, as it rose, it burst into flames and disappeared into space.

"You know the problem I found in that book?" he asked.

Xeno shook his head.

"Remember the ending, where Turnus, leader of an Italian tribe and mortal enemy of the Trojans, is defeated in battle and asks for Aeneas's forgiveness? 'Swallow now your hatred,' he says. Do you remember what Aeneas does?"

"He answers?"

"Yes. And then he plunges his sword into Turnus's chest."

"Well, he deserved it."

"Forgiving him would have shown unprecedented generosity."

"That's true," said Xeno. "I wonder if Virgil ever thought of that."

Coming around a sharp switchback in the road carved into the side of the mountain and talking about the possibility of launching their own spaceship, independent of the great powers—the dream of every astronaut who aspires to be more than a chauffeur of a super-luxury vehicle, as Xeno would say—they saw on the high slope in front of them, small and distant, the figure of a man moving over the rocks.

"But keep the budget in mind," Abdelkrim had said.

Xeno, as if he hadn't heard him, said, "Cooling the heat from the friction is the real problem. But it can also be the solution. Heat is energy, and this would be just the amount required by the thruster."

The little man crouched down. Was he cutting a plant? Or digging? Xeno put the jeep in neutral and stopped at the high end of a gulley.

"He's cutting something. But who is he?"

Abdelkrim took out a pair of binoculars from the glove compartment.

It was a classmate. He recognized him. His name was Matías Pacal, and he specialized in the observation of quasars and pulsars. Abdelkrim passed the binoculars to Xeno.

At that moment, Pacal went from being bathed in the light of the setting sun to being almost swallowed in shadow as the vast curve of night advanced from the horizon. They watched him shift and look toward the southeast before he lay back down on the ground.

Xeno put the binoculars back in the glove compartment.

Abdelkrim's iPod was playing music: the Moroccan rhaita and the darbouka, the small ceramic drums covered with calf membrane played by *djebala* women. The red sky had darkened, and with every second another ten stars rose beyond the mountains to the east.

A gleaming object crossed the space over their heads. Pacal, like Xeno and Abdelkrim, watched it move from north to south in the exosphere. Xeno explained to Abdelkrim, mechanically, that it was a surveillance satellite that circled Earth fourteen times a day in its polar orbit. They too were being observed.

He remembered the talk that Pacal had given on the precise predictions of eclipses in pretechnological societies like the Maya and the Dogon. Afterward at a dinner in his honor, they were introduced. And later, as they walked back to Hotel Avante in downtown Mountain View, Pacal told him that a

Chinese agent had contacted him to work on a space project. They wanted to design rockets capable of placing hundred-pound satellites in a low orbit for under a million dollars.

"That'll go down the toilet before you know it," Xeno predicted, having heard of the project.

"He's in the darkest spot," Xeno said, looking toward the place where the plant cutter was lying on his back.

They got out of the jeep, sand crunching under their sneakers as they walked down the road among agave plants. When they turned to climb up the other side of the gulley, the star-filled sky opened up again over their heads.

Pacal, who heard them coming, waited until they were a few steps away before he stood up. His round face gave off a resinous sheen in the darkness.

"*Salaam aleikum,*" said Abdelkrim, while the other bowed his head slightly.

"Good evening."

Abdelkrim asked if Pacal was looking for something specific.

"No, I was just checking for snakes. I wanted to lie down and look at the sky."

When Pacal was five or six years old in Guatemala, his family lived in a small adobe house in a valley of volcanic origin. There was no public lighting, or even electricity, for many kilometers around. His father, a professor of mechanics in the School of Agronomy in Bárcenas, in the highlands, used to wake the boy before dawn, and they would leave the house when it was still dark enough to see the stars. "'To look at the stars is to look into the past,' my old man used to say," Pacal told them. "He was an atheist. And so am I." They lived very high up, he said, some two thousand meters above sea level, and on moonless nights, the canopy of stars filled young Pacal with religious terror.

"It was frightening," he said, "to see so many stars."

That was 1986, the year the *Challenger* exploded and the year Halley's comet returned. Pacal claimed to have seen the comet in the dark Guatemalan sky with the little telescope his father had given him.

"He's a child of darkness," Xeno later said to Abdelkrim.

At the age of eight, after seeing the photos that the *Voyager* took of Uranus, Pacal decided he would be an astronomer. He read scientific magazines brought home by his father, who encouraged him and helped him with his studies as much as his modest means would allow. His family was poor, closer to the bottom than to the top of the Guatemalan social pyramid. His mother—a rural schoolteacher like his father and a practitioner of Mayan astrology—had died when Pacal was thirteen, but he'd kept her memory alive through force of will. "You'll go very far," she'd prophesied.

After completing his studies, Pacal told them, he entered community college, where he studied pure physics; at that time in Guatemala, astronomy didn't exist as a major. Because of his outstanding grades, he received a fellowship to study astronomy at the Autonomous University of Mexico. A year later, recruited by DARPA (the Defense Advanced Research Projects Agency), he did his internship in Green Bank, West Virginia. When he was about to graduate as a radio astronomer, another headhunter offered him a position at the European Space Agency. From the plains of Westerbork in the Netherlands, his job was to monitor pulsars—neutron stars, remnants of the explosions of supernovas ("the size of Guatemala City," he liked to say), that spin on their axes several hundred times a second, the most powerful magnets in the universe.

"But the ESA began to lose personnel to China, which could pay much more," Pacal had said at the end of his talk at the university. "It became clear that with every foreign project, the researchers would move to countries with more resources and better labs." Yes, and those laboratories, Xeno thought at the time, were funded by big arms manufacturers.

Of all the people he'd had a chance to meet in the New World, Pacal was the strangest, Xeno wrote in an email to his sister, Nada. "The Maya," Pacal used to say, "came to Central America from China thousands of years ago. It was they, not the Spanish, who discovered America." This seemed plausible, given Pacal's own appearance: round, compact, unibrowed. In fact, although light skinned, Pacal looked more Polynesian than Mayan. He knew and could write Chinese (and swore that in Guatemala there were now as many Mandarin- as English-language schools).

Pacal's syncretic religious beliefs, however, were an abomination to Abdelkrim; he tolerated them, as a good Muslim was supposed to, but couldn't take them seriously.

"You give alms to a beggar," Abdelkrim said, mocking Xeno, "and then you wash the hand that touched him."

Xeno wondered if he had inherited this obsession with hygiene from his father. He had certainly seen him do what Abdelkrim described.

"It is written," the Moroccan would say, "that we who follow the true faith are obliged to understand, to tolerate, and to trust that with the help of Allah, we can persuade those who have not had the good fortune to grow in our faith, that they might receive the milk and honey of Islam—sweeter than the finest honey, more delicious than a mother's milk."

They squatted down on the ground like Bedouins. All that was missing was the tea, Xeno said. Then he mentioned a possible ancestor of Pacal: Pacal the Great, whose sarcophagus was discovered in the Temple of Inscriptions in Palenque. Some people called him the Mayan cosmonaut. Pacal laughed—he rejected the idea of any relation. Next, they talked about the possibility of space voyages that would not depend on the combustion of fossil fuels and nuclear power—methods such as had been used by . . . by whom? A system, maybe, that would use water as fuel to reach outer space, and then liquid oxygen.

"Wouldn't it be possible," Pacal had suggested, "to use a volcano as a cauldron in which water could be converted into energy?"

"Now we are really *mkiyif*!" Abdelkrim commented.

Instead of being shocked by the ideas that divided them—the Sunni Muslim, the Greek Orthodox Christian, and the Guatemalan atheist—they had taken the heavens above them as a point of reference in relation to which they could be almost equals.

"For us," Abdelkrim said after another surveillance satellite had passed over their heads, "a certain type of ignorance is necessary to reach a state of grace. You two can take charge of designing the machine and drawing up the maps. I'll handle the flying and navigation."

Pacal looked up at the sky. No one said anything.

"Our mission, our cause," Xeno continued, "will be to disable as many satellite systems as possible—low orbit, medium, and geostationary. And after that, or perhaps at the same time, to dismantle the principal transoceanic cable connections. In short, to create chaos. To offset the damage done, and to prevent further damage by other nation-states, we'll need to go back several centuries, technically speaking."

"Our cause is chaos?" said Pacal.

They dropped him off at Hotel Avante.

"We'll have to stay in touch," he said in parting, "so we can keep talking about how to destroy the world."

It was the first time Xeno had seen him smile.

IV

The last winter he spent in Patmos, Xeno was plagued by doubts. Although religious faith seemed necessary to him, it did not seem sufficient, as he told the abbot when he visited. The old man was stretched out on what they both knew would be his deathbed.

"You could take my place, if you wanted to," the abbot said, gripping Xeno's hand. Nodding, Xeno squeezed his hand in return.

The island was almost deserted. The hills, very green and mantled here and there with red poppies or daisies, vibrated between the blue of the sky and, in the background, the blue of the sea. Too much beauty, Xeno thought, for too sad a day. For no reason, he remembered a poor neighborhood in Boston he'd visited when he had first gone to MIT. Now, walking through the narrow alleys among the whitewashed stone houses of Khora on his way back from the Byzantine stronghold, Xeno, as he'd done since childhood, avoided stepping on the spaces between the slabs. He walked hurriedly, though there was no reason to—he had nowhere to be—and his steps clapped on the stones like the beats of a tabla.

"Not to lie, not to kill, and to give to those in need." These were the last words he heard the abbot say.

All actions—good, bad, even indifferent—have a double effect. What had been the aim of his actions lately? He felt, with the sudden force of a revelation, that he had a special task to complete during his residency on Earth. He felt goose bumps, a sensation that bordered on the voluptuous, and then a shudder. Was it the spirit of the other—the person who'd just died—that had entered him?

The rhythm of walking had cheered him, and he had an easy slope ahead of him. Perhaps he was giving in to arrogance. Perhaps to feel what he was feeling, it was necessary to see things from on high. "One should not expect God to come from the earth but from heaven," Saint John had written. Couldn't he, Xeno, two thousand years later, transform his own world from heaven? Wasn't it possible, he wondered, looking at the sea from a bend in the path, to overcome evil from time to time? Below him he saw a half-broken old dovecote with several doves cooing and flying around it. Shouldn't it be possible, at least, to end *physical* violence? (Suffering was another matter; perhaps it could never have an end.) Buddha, Jesus, even Marx must have felt something like this. *I could fail too,* he said to himself, and at that moment the monastery bells—five different sizes of bells—of Saint John the Theologian rang out. It was as if the melody, familiar as an old toy, had transported him to a new dimension. He felt it the way animals feel such things, with a shiver.

He stopped at a little convenience store to buy fruits and vegetables before going home. On the front page of a newspaper, he saw a photo of an old, dark-skinned African man lying on the beach, wearing white pants and a red T-shirt. The photo was artfully composed: the man was stretched out on the cream-colored sand between two patrolmen dressed in black, under a cloudless sky on the island of Kos. "Drowned man surprises tourists," the caption said.

It was not acceptable that in the present day there should be *so much* material suffering. A certain former trafficker of pirated videos born in Jordan, a drug user with the aura of a loser, had founded a bloody caliphate (prompted, as everyone knew, by US military action in Iraq) that fomented religious massacres and that had spread with a success as implacable as it was unforeseen. In the space of only a year, threatened by the meteoric success of the new caliphate, almost a million people had fled Syria and Iraq to seek refuge in Europe. Today, the most powerful nations on Earth could not contain its expansion or guarantee the safety of their own citizens. None of this seemed mysterious to Xeno. The arms industry resembled the mythical Uroboros, the enormous serpent that devours itself tail first. The making and selling of weapons had become necessary to sustain the economies of powerful nations (the US, Britain, Russia, France, Germany, and the others) and to maintain the lifestyle of the people who lived in these nations, people who were accustomed to feeling protected by their governments, irrespective of their ideologies. In order for these economies not to collapse, the powerful had to sell weapons to their enemies, enemies they could no longer control, who were attacking them for ideological reasons. The image of the collective suicide of the human race passed through his head. Someone had written that the works of man would be the cause of his extinction. Xeno hadn't forgotten:

> *Out of the depths of secret caverns, beings will arise to sow danger and death, leaving mankind prostrate with suffering. Those who submit to the law of these beings, after much sacrifice, will find momentary pleasure. But those who fail to pay them homage will find only agony and death. These beings will make men wretched; they will incite them to betray and to steal from each other. They will cause men to distrust those nearest to them. They will reduce free cities to slavery. O vile monsters! How much better were it for men that you shouldst return to hell!*

Leonardo was speaking here, enigmatically, of *metals*. And man, Xeno thought, who had extracted these metals from the earth, was annihilating himself at the same time that he launched these metals into the heavens. "And the dead would no doubt be many more in number," the Florentine wrote in yet another riddle, referring to armor, "if other soulless beings did not emerge from the bowels of the earth to defend them."

V

In 2014, a Russian space agency had proposed a system to eliminate a great deal of the space garbage floating in low and medium orbits around Earth, propelling it into a "graveyard" orbit far beyond the geostationary. From there, space carcasses would spiral outward, drifting farther and farther from Earth. According to the agency, the system would cost about three billion dollars. It was on the basis of this idea that Xeno conceived his own project, demented in appearance but achievable. Neither the arms manufacturers nor their clients would be able to survive the revolution that, with the help of luck and a circle of friends, Xeno planned to set in motion.

His project—his *mission*—was to create three vast rings of destruction around the planet. A single spaceship stationed at one of the Lagrangian points—the points where a small object, by virtue of gravity, can maintain its position in outer space with respect to two larger bodies, such as Earth and the moon—could do the work that Xeno envisaged: a small technological apocalypse in the low and medium orbits and then, afterward, in the geostationary. "The Rings of Earth," Xeno had said, feeling inspired. The ship would be equipped with a small radio telescope, like the Hubble but much less powerful, made not to detect pulsars and quasars but to locate and pursue satellites of various kinds—communications or surveillance, including AWACS (airborne warning and control system). "Automatic target recognition," Pacal quoted. "With a medium-power laser, it'll work."

"We need to try it out," Xeno had said that night in the desert. The word *apocatastasis* flashed before his eyes.

"What about a nuclear detonation at a certain point in the synchronic orbit, to create an electromagnetic pulse? That would do more damage in less time," Abdelkrim suggested. "And it would be less expensive."

Xeno objected. To begin with, he didn't want to use nuclear weapons. Besides, whoever detonated the bomb would be condemned to death. This was not the message he wanted to convey.

"But think of the budget," Abdelkrim repeated. He was suggesting that he would be willing to sacrifice himself.

Xeno shook his head. He didn't approve of this kind of martyrdom.

It would be his great accomplishment: the Rings of Earth.

They would have to disable hundreds of satellites—worth between a hundred million and a billion dollars each—in the space of twenty-four hours. This idea would turn *him* into a martyr, he said to himself with a certain pious thrill, as he looked out at the sea from his garden terrace.

First they'd have to obtain the essential components: the ship's carbon-fiber frame and its ceramic, temperature-resistant covering; layers of fireproof material; the engine; the air reactor; and the oxygen cooler—the most complicated part of all (it would have to cool the air, in a fraction of a second, from 1,000 degrees to 150). They would take all the components to Turkey—perhaps—or to Mexico to reassemble them, he imagined, in some well-funded museum as part of an exhibit of "space art." A performance. Something like the erection of the cigar-shaped Skylon in London in 1951.

"In spite of the rain, I like Patmos better in winter," he wrote to his mother, who insisted he take the ferry to Piraeus and spend New Year's Eve in Athens with the family.

VI

That spring Xeno received his doctorate in fluid mechanics from Stanford University. Toward the end of May of the same year, while laid over in Madrid on his flight from Boston to Athens, he read a story called "An Asian Fable" in a Spanish magazine. It was also the year the Chinese project that Pacal had worked on fell apart—as Xeno had predicted it would.

Xeno's mother was planning a banquet for a group of summer vacationers, some of them owners of houses on Patmos, some of them possible buyers—or sellers—of very, very expensive art, and also the usual friends.

Mrs. Galanis had gotten up that day in an excellent mood. She sent Assia, her Bulgarian cook, by taxi to look for fish at Grikos, a fishing village. Now she was going over the guest list. She had a mental diagram in front of her, and she was arranging guests around the imaginary table according to a mix of

considerations, advantages, and probabilities. She asked Xeno
to help her make the confirmation calls.

There would be twenty-two guests.

"Counting the four of us," she said, "that's twenty-six."

There were two last-minute cancellations.

Xeno approached the stairwell and heard his mother in
the kitchen, speaking affably with Assia, who had just come
back from Grikos with three sea bream of four pounds each,
the catch of the day.

"Efharistó."

"Parakaló."

"Marina and the duke aren't coming!"

"Why not?"

"They can't," Xeno said.

This produced a silence.

"Call Eleni. She's here with her new boyfriend or whatever
he is. A Central African. His name is Homer—can you imagine? Why not? Bangui is the capital, right?"

Xeno nodded from the top of the stairs, and his mother
recited Eleni's number from memory.

A few minutes later Eleni confirmed. "Can I bring something?" she asked through SMS.

"Diamonds. Or an elephant tusk," Xeno suggested.

"Bad joke," Eleni replied.

Xeno reviewed the guest list:

- A Greek princess, her French companion, and their Argentinian friend: confirmed.
- An Italian collector (without his wife): confirmed.
- A plastic surgeon from Los Angeles and his Swiss multimillionaire boyfriend: confirmed.
- A former French minister and his Greek lover: confirmed.
- A Majorcan artist: pending.
- The neighbors (an illustrator of large cats in their natural habitat and her husband, a retired mining geologist): confirmed.
- A Finnish architect and his wife, a gallerist: confirmed.
- A Turkish photographer and his teenage daughter: confirmed.
- An English heiress and her husband, an Austrian collector: confirmed.
- A Venezuelan heiress: confirmed.
- A Greek adventurer and scientist: pending.
- An Italian industrialist (owner of the longest yacht in the world): confirmed.

VII

Intelligence agents following the trail of activities connected to ISIS report that certain Turkish elements are engaged in recruiting young minds to radicalize them. "Our biggest threat consists of academics who may be affiliated with ISIS. They're in touch with cadres in Turkey," the agent declared. (Interesting.)

ISIS preaches the theology of rape. Victims once again provide details of abuses against women and children, seen as a form of prayer to Allah—said the front page of the *International New York Times.* (Unlikely.)

Hundreds of drowned immigrants on the coasts of Kos, Leros, and Kalymnos. (Unacceptable.)

Mexican tourists dead in Egypt: bombed in an air raid. This Sunday, police and the Egyptian Army killed Mexican tourists while pursuing Jihadists. (*Inevitable,* thought Xeno.)

VIII

Lowering his voice, Xeno said to Iris, the teenager, "Do they know what's going on in Leros?"

"What can they do about it?" she asked.

Xeno's mother shot them an inquisitive look.

Keeping his voice low, Xeno asked the girl, "How could it occur to my mom to invite a Central African and then prohibit any talk of politics?"

Then, in full voice, so that everyone could hear, "I wonder how much a kilo of ivory is worth today. Two thousand euros? Three?"

His mother got up from the table, saying she was going to bring the coffee. "And the Majorcan? Not even the courtesy of a reply, thank you very much," she said. "He's a monster, I've been told. I'd like to have met him."

The Central African, a figure out of Goya, raised his arms and exclaimed, "If my friends could see me here tonight"—he looked around the table, grinning—"with all of you! Just me and a few of my men—an easy job." He looked at the girl. "In your case, well, we'd let you go, of course. But think of it: one single blow and we'd change the course of history. All those refugees! A humanitarian Trojan horse, eh? Why not?"

Everyone was horrified. Working himself up, the Central African went on raving to the guests around the table—all of them silent.

Over the monastery wall, directly above the house in Khora, Xeno could see a monk looking out at the horizon toward Asia Minor. Was he waiting for a signal?

Nikolaos Pontekorvo, the scientist adventurer, questioned the Central African man. "And what exactly do you do in Bangui?"

"Me? I've done everything—even kidnapping."

"Between June and December of 2015, some seven hundred thousand refugees crossed the Mediterranean, most of them landing quite near these coasts. Three thousand seven hundred died before they reached the shore," Xeno's father said.

"Money," Nick was saying. "There's plenty of it. At this table alone . . ."

Mrs. Galanis, standing at the kitchen door, protested.

"We'll talk later," said Nick.

Nada, Xeno's sister, got up from her chair and approached Xeno. She asked that he not leave her out of the plot they seemed to be hatching. The Venezuelan woman also came up to Xeno—another one who wanted to be included. Xeno closed his eyes and agreed.

"There are people who don't believe in giving if they can sell," said Nick.

And then, when Mrs. Galanis returned to the table, he said, "This is the best fish I've eaten in Patmos, I swear. By the way," he said to Xeno, "that plan, One Laptop per Child, was meant for India. And yes, they torpedoed it. The thing is still possible, as it always was, at least technically. Weapons are still the best business, of course."

He proposed a toast to Xeno's mother, and everyone except the teenager raised their cups and glasses.

Xeno looked at Iris.

"I'm superstitious," she said without smiling. "One shouldn't toast without alcohol."

"The situation is much more complicated," Xeno began to explain to Alex, the geologist seated to his right. "The low and high orbits around Earth have become focal points of activity. They're full of hundreds of satellites from some seventy different countries. Their purposes might be peaceful, scientific, or commercial, but all of them are at risk. Not all the members of the growing club of space powers are inclined to play by the same rules—and they don't really have to, since the rules don't exist."

The Central African turned to Xeno and said, "They say they want to prevent 'any possible attack on the satellite systems of the United States and its allies'"—he opened and closed the quotes with his fingers—"while they feel free to go on bombing our cities and killing our people en masse."

Nick changed the subject again. He turned to the gallerist, Ana, who seemed bored sitting between the surgeon and the princess.

"How is the art business?"

"I can't complain. Yesterday I sold a Frans Hals over the phone."

"*The Fisher Boy*?"

"Yes!"

Mrs. Galanis raised her eyebrows. At her table, talk of politics and religion was strictly forbidden. If she had her way, she would exclude sales talk as well, she said.

"For six million," Iris whispered at almost the same time.

Evidently a rebellion was afoot.

The Venezuelan said to Iris, "Six million! How do you know?"

"It was on Instagram," Xeno explained.

"Last fall in New York, a nude by Modigliani sold for a hundred and seventy million—over the phone—to a Chinese taxi magnate," Ana reminded them.

IX

"It's just a matter of finding witnesses now," read the coded message Xeno sent to Abdelkrim from the house in Khora some months later.

"Tomorrow I'll fly from Guatemala to Tangier, via Panama and Madrid," Abdelkrim answered, using the same code.

On the kitchen table, beside the figs cut up and arranged by Assia on a platter from the isle of Sifnos, someone had left a copy of the *International New York Times*. Another Syrian refugee drowned. Another attack of indignation. He reached for a fig. The sweet taste and mealy texture filled his mouth.

On Patmos one could be *too* content, he thought with a slightly guilty conscience, unusual for him. A faint sense of shame—he remembered the phrase from Adorno—at the fact of still having a little air to breathe in hell.

PART THREE

Infection

"You should know," said the philosopher, "that at this moment, as I speak to you, there are a hundred thousand madmen with hats or helmets on their heads, who are killing another hundred thousand brutes with turbans on their heads—or letting themselves be killed by them—and that, all over the planet, this is how we pass our time."

With a shudder, the Syrian inquired as to the reason for such horrible fighting.

—Voltaire, *Micromégas*

I

They used to say in Tangier that one of the traditions of the US Secret Service was to place an agent at the head of the Old American Legation, located in the lower eastern side of the medina. The new director, David Singer—six foot two, well built, bald, macrocephalic—was no exception. He could have stepped out of a Graham Greene novel, the Mexican thought when they were introduced after a colloquium on Tangerine Darija at the book fair. A native of New Jersey, habitually smiling but harsh voiced, Singer had managed to erase almost any trace of an American accent from his markedly peninsular Spanish. He spoke classic Arabic as fluently as Darija, and he was interested in Moroccan music and cooking. He seemed pleased by the fact that everyone assumed he worked for the CIA, though whenever someone asked him about it, he didn't know how to respond.

"What can somebody in my shoes say, apart from the fact that if it were true, I'd have to deny it?" he had said to the Mexican.

The museum of the Old Legation was a two-hundred-year-old building that took up both sides of the rue d'Amérique, above which an elevated walkway connected the two. The doorkeeper didn't recognize the Mexican from years before, when he used to frequent the library. After asking for identification, he pointed the way—by means of corridors, a stairway, and a small courtyard—to Singer's office.

The Mexican explained to Singer that he needed help reading some documents in classical Arabic.

"They're from a Moroccan boy, from Tangier—studying in Boston, it seems," he added.

Singer said he knew who the boy was. He asked if the Mexican had the text with him.

"But how is it you know who he is?" he asked.

"His father has managed to make it public," Singer said without concealing his disapproval. "He tells everyone that his son will be the first Moroccan astronaut. But this is not at all certain, no, sir."

The visitor took the memory card out of his pants pocket and handed it to the American spy, who promptly inserted it into his computer.

"We've got a problem," he said after pressing keys and making clicking sounds on the French keyboard. He took out the card and returned it to the Mexican. "The card is formatted for a Mac. This is a PC."

The Mexican told him he had a Mac laptop in his backpack.

"Perfect! I've got the afternoon free," said Singer, in a better mood. "And the night too! I like this. Let's get started."

The Mexican followed him through the old, labyrinthine building. They went up a narrow staircase, across the elevated walkway, and then down another spiral staircase; they crossed a patio with a tiled fountain and entered a small library.

"Did you know Field?" Singer asked.

"A little."

"Well, it's an honor to meet someone who knew that great man. Please, make yourself at home. Can we use *tú*?"

They sat down in front of a black wooden desk that took up half the room; the high walls were lined with shelves stacked with dictionaries and old books bound in various colors of Moroccan leather.

The desktop that appeared on the Mac looked as if a bewildering memory game had opened up: it was an image of the disordered mental world of his friend, the small and tenacious Carrie.

"It's not mine," he said. "It's a friend's."

David Singer looked at the apparatus with an ambiguous expression.

"I don't much like Macs," he said.

"Neither do I," the other replied as he slipped in the card. "I'm PC too."

II

"It's a letter," said Singer, "addressed to the imams of Emsallah and Souani." He began to take notes. Then he got up from the desk and stood on a stool to take down an old multilingual dictionary from a shelf. He opened it on the desk and began to leaf through it.

"Excuse me," he said. "Just a moment. But this boy knows how to write. That is, if he really wrote this."

~

Brothers and Sisters!

Let us learn, as Allah wishes, to work well, to think well, to live well. Let us raise our eyes to heaven before lowering them again to the Book to read, so that the divine light and no other will help us interpret what is written there. It is not easy to understand! When you speak to parents who have children to educate, do you think they understand the complexity of the world?

Out of love and fear of Allah the all-powerful, the merciful, he who knows all and sees all, who is the witness of our deeds and the judge of our sins, let us not deceive ourselves. Nothing displeases the Lord more than the tyranny of man over man, and for tyrants—so says the Book—there is a special place.

Al-lah hu a'lam. *He can count the sands of the desert!*

∽

Underneath a cartoon of three Arab leaders looking at each other with hostility, the caption, which Singer translated, read: *The enemies of my enemies are my enemies.*

∽

How much importance shall we allot to some infantile and malicious drawings? Is it just and fair to be offended by something like this? Is it right to think that a cartoon should be taken seriously, that it could somehow stain the glory of the Most High?

∽

In Harran, my brothers, there is no fresh water. Do you know where Harran is? Well then. The earth in Harran is an oven that heats everything. There is no shade in which to rest, the air burns your nostrils and your lungs. Have you been there? Harran is a forgotten land. Nothing lives well there, and yet for its sake, men fight today, our enemies and our brothers . . .

"He's quoting Maalouf," said Singer, "who's quoting Ibn Jaldún in turn . . . or maybe Ibn Yubair. But he's speaking of today's Harran," he added in an appreciative tone. "It's obvious."

The computer said seven o'clock. They'd been working almost three hours. One could hear the voice of the muezzin calling the Maghreb. Almost all the legation staff had left.

"What time do you close?" the Mexican asked.

Singer was still reading, without translating, the next paragraph. He took off his glasses and said, "If you want, we can stay here all night—working."

He felt that Singer's interest in Abdelkrim's letters was excessive. "I'm afraid I'd better go," he said. "I've got a dinner engagement." (*Is Singer really an agent?* he kept asking himself.)

"OK. Perhaps we can copy the card?"

"I don't think so."

Singer closed his eyes; they moved under his eyelids. He opened them and said, "My friend, perhaps you don't understand me. As a US citizen, I consider it my duty to know what's on this card. It contains something that could well be related to a radical organization.

"And I think," he added in English, "you know exactly what I mean. It is my duty to share this immediately with our consulate."

Our? thought the Mexican. He closed the laptop and stood up.

Singer's attitude changed.

"Look. Before doing anything official, anything dramatic, wouldn't it be best just to finish transcribing what we have here?" He pointed to the Mexican's pants pocket where he had just put the card. "Don't you think so? After all, it could be just the diatribe of a bigheaded student who thinks he's going to explain the Koran to the imams."

"Diatribe?" the Mexican said.

"I propose that we keep on working tomorrow morning. What time shall we say?" asked Singer, typing the Mexican's number on his cell phone. "I'll just dial it so you'll have my number too. There. Perfect." He smiled. "Do you think you can get that again?" he asked, pointing to the computer.

The Mexican wiped off a few droplets of the saliva that sprayed his face.

The word *infection* crossed his mind. "It's possible," he said.

Singer got up to leave by the hallway door, and the Mexican followed him. He was more than a head taller than the Mexican, and his shoulders seemed packed with muscle. They turned down the very narrow hallway by which they had come, went up a short flight of stairs, turned down another hallway, and crossed the bridge over the little street of the medina. Now they stood in a courtyard, much wider than the others and accessible via another spiral staircase. Singer stopped to look at the Mexican.

"Is it true that you knew Field well?"

He had already told him he knew Field only briefly. He said so again.

"Look," Singer said, and invited him into a small sitting room. On the walls hung various photographs of the painter. "A little homage to a great traveler and an equally great artist. As I told you, it's an honor for me to know someone who knew him. Have you already seen these photos?"

He gestured to them: Field with his wife, Lynn; with Mohammed Mrabet and Ahmed Yacoubi; with the Bowleses; with Claudio Bravo; with Miquel Barceló and Claude Nathalie Thomas; with Cherie Nutting; and with Mohammed Zhrouni.

While the Mexican was absorbed in the photos, Singer went out to the courtyard to text on his iPhone 6. After viewing the photos, the Mexican closely examined a map drawn in the 1960s by Field himself, which showed the locations of the *tchars* in the Atlas Mountains, where he had done some of his cloud paintings. Singer was still texting rapidly. Once again, the word *infection* ran through the Mexican's head. Singer had drawn him into the room full of photos to distract him. Now other agents would know of the existence of that card, which seemed to Singer so suspicious, and they would know who the bearer was. *Are they going to hunt me down?* he wondered. He felt a pang at his temples, an unpleasant tingling of the skin behind his knees. He went out to the courtyard; Singer stopped texting.

"Interesting, aren't they?" Singer said, referring to a series of photos of the Maghreb sky at certain hours of the morning and afternoon.

They crossed the courtyard and strolled toward the door to the street. The doorkeeper, who had been dozing, stood up from his stool and opened the old, very heavy door.

III

He turned left to go down the little street that led out of the medina. After a few steps he stopped and turned on his heels. He retraced the short path he'd taken and walked past the front door of the legation again. Then he began to walk quickly down the street, which plunged into the noisy and colorful labyrinth of the old medina. He was frightened, certain now that someone, maybe several men, would come after him to get the laptop and memory card.

Every house, every corner of the network of small streets, was part of a landscape from his past, familiar yet at the same time terrifying. He remembered, in spurts, moments from his childhood. They say that when the fox is on the run, he enjoys the thrill and danger of the chase as much as the pack of hounds and the hunters—as if it were a game. He walked quickly, sometimes breaking into a run. The game was to hide among the people or in the cranny of some wall so that he could look behind him. *I'm going crazy,* he thought.

Shaken by his discovery, and uneasy at having stood up to Singer—the supposed agent—he turned down a street of jewelry shops, toward the Zoco Chico. Then he climbed up the Calle de los Nazarenos. *Our street,* he thought (though this seemed absurd to him under the circumstances), lengthening his stride, the backpack holding the laptop on his shoulders. He turned again up a little curved street with no visible name— Cordoneros?—and then back down a wider street until he reached the Plaza Dar Baroud, the old arsenal, and finally Calle de las Babuchas. He stopped in front of a bazaar from whose doors hung clusters of slippers of various colors and sizes. He looked around. A few paces away stood a meek-looking old man—white bearded, tall, slender. Seeing the Mexican standing there, the man said in Spanish, "Looking for something, *sidi*? Come in. I have things I think you'll like."

Behind the old man hung a row of djellabas of apparently good quality.

The street was empty. He walked into the shop, trusting that no one would see him go in.

He chose a cream-colored djellaba. On seeing himself in the rusty mirror that the old man held in front of him, he thought he didn't look bad. Then he chided himself for indulging in such vanity at a time like this.

"Enta tanjaoui!" said the old man, smiling in seeming complicity.

"Iyeh?"

They had barely negotiated the price, but he was ready to leave the shop, satisfied with his purchase, his disguise.

"Shukran b'sef."

"Al-lah-yau nik."

He turned two or three corners, headed up again toward the casbah, and walked into a small restaurant next to Bab el-Assa. He sat inside, asked for a mint tea, and then went to the bathroom, down in a narrow basement that smelled of urine and humidity. A couple of large flies orbited around the hole in the floor. He took off the djellaba and opened up the backpack. He extracted the laptop and stuck it between his abdomen and his belt. Out of the top pocket of the backpack, he took out his passport (which he'd carried with him since that morning when he'd had to go to the bank to get cash). *"Hamdul-lah,"* he said in a soft voice. Having the passport with him gave him a feeling of security that he needed now. He tucked the passport in the inside breast pocket of his jacket and buttoned it tight.

He decided to get rid of the backpack. He emptied it completely—glasses and case, a pack of chewing gum, a Swiss Army knife, a notebook, a pen—and put all the contents into the pockets of his jacket. He put on his djellaba again. He rolled the backpack into a ball and stuffed it, with difficulty, into the bottom of the little trash can of the restroom, which he then covered up with a layer of toilet paper. The precautions, probably unnecessary, calmed him; when he got back to his table, he felt fairly sure that nobody was following him.

He drank some of his tea, paid his bill, and then, shifting the computer under his belt to keep it in place, joined the many Tangerines and tourists passing through the casbah. He was less troubled now but still alert to any sign of a pursuer.

He went down the Calle de Italia until he reached the Zoco de Fuera, where he found a taxi.

In Tangier there are two kinds of taxis. The petits taxis are coupes, painted blue with a horizontal band of egg yellow; the grands taxis are white- or cream-colored Mercedes-Benzes. Most people considered it a sign of arrogance to sit in the back seat as Europeans usually do. The Mexican took a petit taxi and sat in front.

Instead of asking the driver to take him to Hotel Atlas, where he was staying, he said, "Grand Hotel Villa de France, please."

"Where?"

"You don't know it?"

"Where is it?"

"The corner of Inglaterra and Holanda."

"Certainly."

He decided he didn't want to take any risks. He would pay for the five-star hotel for one night.

They drove uphill along Bou Araquía, the street that borders the Muslim cemetery. It was an unnecessary detour, but he said nothing. The ancient, long wall of the cemetery, where beggars used to sit, had been demolished, and now the merchants of pity had to practice their trade elsewhere; the lamentations of their *liara* and their *qsbahs* were a thing of the past.

. "Excuse me," he said to the driver, and began to remove the djellaba. The driver looked at him out of the corner of his eye.

"*Makein mushkil.* No problem, *sidi.*"

His phone began to ring. By the time he got the djellaba off, he'd lost the call. Singer's number appeared on the screen. He left it alone.

With the djellaba rolled up under his arm and the computer still under his shirt, he crossed the parking lot of the Grand Hotel Villa de France and went down the stairs toward the patio with the fountain and the arches.

He hadn't been to the hotel in a long time. It had closed around 1993 after losing one star. An Iraqi company had then bought it and remodeled it. At the new reception desk, he felt strange. The bulldozer of time had demolished the old lobby. In place of the threadbare Berber rugs, the floor was covered with modern carpeting, and the Andalusian stucco and ceramic mosaics had been replaced by imitation marble and mirrors. On one of the walls was a poster reproducing Matisse's *Paysage vu d'une fenêtre*. The new proprietors boasted of having preserved—in one of the third-floor rooms—the window from which Matisse saw this view of Tangier. The Mexican contemplated the reproduction with its flat perspective and bold colors: the walls of Saint Andrew's church, the gardens and the plaza of the Mendubía. The receptionist, a tall, young Moroccan woman affecting French manners, told him that the Matisse room was available for no additional cost. Now that the book fair was over, the hotel was empty.

"I'll take it."

"*Trés bien, monsieur.* Your passport, please."

He showed her his passport and handed her his credit card.

"*Voilà,*" she said, giving him an electronic key and the password for the internet. "Matisse1912," he read on the little strip of paper.

"*Bonne nuit, monsieur. Pas de valise?*"

"*Non. Merci.*"

He was looking out at the Tangier night through the celebrated window, mentally comparing the master's painting with the scene that lay before his eyes, when the ring of his phone brought him sharply back to the present. It was eight thirty.

"Hello," the Mexican said dully.

It was Singer.

"Ah, I'm glad to catch you. I called you just a moment ago. Am I bothering you?"

"No."

"Honestly?"

"Honestly."

"Are you at your hotel?"

"Yes," he half lied.

"The Atlas, yes?"

He preferred not to answer.

"Good. Look. After you left, I thought more about that computer. Don't worry, I found another Mac."

"Perfect."

"OK, eleven o'clock tomorrow morning, then. Don't you want me to come by and pick you up at the hotel?"

"No, thanks."

"Very well. Look . . ."

He looked down at the little phone with the desire to hang up.

"I need you to understand now," Singer went on. "I've done a little research . . . This kid, Abdelkrim . . ."

"Uh-huh."

"Well, he might be involved in something"—his voice lowered several tones—"very delicate. I'd rather not talk about it over the phone. Tomorrow I'll give you the details. OK?"

"OK. It's getting kind of late for me. Excuse me."

"Yeah. Have a great dinner. You're sure you don't want me to swing by and get you in the morning?"

"No, thanks very much."

"Good night."

"Yes. Good night to you too."

After hanging up, he dialed Carrie's number. Boujeloud answered. The Mexican asked him to come by in the morning and pick up the laptop.

"I'm not at the Atlas now," he explained. "I'm staying at the Villa de France. Can you come a little before eleven?"

"Ouakha, Ouakha."

He opened the laptop and connected to the internet. He looked through his email; there was nothing urgent to answer. An article of his about Central American drug traffickers was going to be published in *El País*; his Spanish editor congratulated him. A column that he had published in *Vanity Fair* a month before had received, as of this moment, only five "likes." Disgruntled, he read it over again:

An Asian Fable

I'm traveling through Europe with my twelve-year-old goddaughter and one of her friends from high school, so I must update my learning. But during an after-dinner conversation of the kind one often has on such trips, I find myself at a loss to explain the difference between human intelligence and what may seem like intel-ligence in machines. I present two or three arguments that, I'm afraid, don't manage to convince the girls, who have just read, in Paris, a text called *Identifying Humanoids: A User's Guide*, a pamphlet for a questionable product called Somatic Design, accompanied by this note: "This leaflet contains basic information on the interaction of humans with imitation humanoids in 3D." A joke, obviously, but it's alarming, most of all because the girls seem to have taken it seriously.

A few days later, a likely illustration of a peculiar aspect of human intelligence comes to me in a dream.

It was one of those dreams in which the dreamer is a neutral entity, bodiless, a mere spectator. We find ourselves on the Mediterranean coast of Syria, in a landscape of white sand, blue sea, and men dressed in black. A group of illegal immigrants is about to board a barge, to escape a mob of militia—are they ISIS? In the group there are five children without parents; they'll be the last to come aboard. A dilemma arises: there is space for only three of them. A decision needs to be made: Who will be left behind on the beach?

If the problem were presented to a machine or to an adult mind, the solution would be simple: luck or caprice would dictate the outcome. But it so happens that the children—who had become the best of friends on the journey that brought them from a city slum (it might have been in Aleppo or Tadmur) all the way to the coast—are the ones who must solve the problem. At the end of a brief discussion, the children turn to the captain of the barge to give the only humane response possible: they're not willing to play that game. They will stay together on the beach. The adults are exasperated. The children stick to their decision. The captain gives the order to set sail. As the boat moves out to sea and the waves grow larger and larger, the children see a cloud of dust rising on the horizon inland. It might be the genocidal militias approaching. The five children at that moment become the secret and privileged guardians of something exclusively ours—the human essence—and which, like a sense of the absolute, can sometimes be communicated through words.

In the darkness of the little Parisian hotel, newly awakened from a dream turning to nightmare, I think: the destiny of the adults who set out over the rough sea, though at first sight better than what lies in store for the children—who are now burying themselves in the sand—is as uncertain as any other human destiny. But the children's destiny is more certain. The decision they have just made on that Syrian beach (or is it only in the dream?) has made them heroic and thus immortal.

He went down for a light dinner in the hotel restaurant. The waiter who served him was an old man who seemed to him strangely familiar. He knew him, in fact. Many years ago, someone had pointed him out, claiming he was an informer. He didn't care for the way the man was staring at him now.

That night he had another strange dream. A guide was leading him through a kind of planetary museum. At a certain moment, the guide left him alone, but he could still hear his voice—smooth, explanatory. He opened his eyes without quite waking up, and he could see a bird hovering in front of the window. The voice came from this bird, he thought, still in the dream; its eyes were two points of red light. *Or is it a drone?* he asked himself, startled. He awoke.

Shroud

I

It was after seven thirty in the morning. From the Matisse window, he could see the deep and luminous blue sky and hear the clear cries of a bird—was it a crow? Now, in the morning light, his fears and suspicions seemed exaggerated, even absurd. David Singer was not a secret agent; he was merely doing his duty as a citizen and a functionary of the American empire. It was normal that he would see something alarming in Abdelkrim's words, that they'd make him think he was connected with an enemy, even one as fearsome as ISIS. Singer would not, on account of that, have had him followed in order to seize Carrie's computer and Abdelkrim's memory card.

There was something left to read on the card, and Singer was eager to help him with that task. If they found evidence of a possible connection with a terrorist or subversive organization, well, he'd let Singer take matters into his own hands. He would limit himself to letting Mohammed know (he would find a way) and would go ahead with his trip, perhaps that same day.

He called room service to have a continental breakfast brought to his room. After finishing it, he stayed awhile, absorbed, watching the Moroccan sky, the Bay of Tangier, the gardens of Saint Andrew and the Mendubía. He decided to walk over to Hotel Atlas to shower and change before meeting Boujeloud and going down to the medina. As a precaution— surely unnecessary, he thought—he hid Carrie's laptop in his pillowcase and hung the little "Do Not Disturb" sign on the door as he left the room.

On Calle de Fez he stopped to buy newspapers—*El País*, *Libération*, and *Al-Alam*, a new Moroccan daily—and took a stroll down Calle de Abd-el-Nassr. As usual, a beggar, who everyone said had lost an arm and a leg twenty years ago in the war against the Polisario Front, sat there. As a compensation for his loss, the Moroccan government allowed him to sell kif and hashish on the public thoroughfare. Even though smoking made the Mexican a little paranoid, he wanted to perform the North African ritual once again.

"Salaam aleikum."

"Aleikum salaam."

"Culshi m'sien?"

"Hamdul-lah."

Out of courtesy, the Mexican was in the habit of exchanging a few words with the man before he asked for the goods.

"Somebody's following you," said Sultán—that's what everyone called the man. "Don't look back. A boy is watching you—white pants, yellow shirt. Better not buy anything now, my friend."

"Are you sure?"

He let a few coins fall to the ground as if by accident; he crouched down to pick them up, so as to cast a look in the direction Sultán had indicated. A boy fitting the beggar's description stood there, on the corner of Calle de Fez, one street down, showing a studious lack of interest. It looked as if he were using a knife to write something on the pitted wall.

"Thank you."

He handed some coins to Sultán, who thanked him without enthusiasm.

"For a coffee," he said.

"Thanks, friend."

He turned the corner and went up Moussa Ben Noussair toward the hotel. Before going in, he looked in all directions. He didn't see the boy; anyway, they already knew where he was staying, he thought. He went up to his room, shrouded in fear.

Who was after him? *It's absurd,* he said to himself again. He shouldn't let them intimidate or manipulate him. He wouldn't go back to the legation—any excuse would suffice. He would go and make a copy of the memory card, just in case. Then he would visit Mohammed.

He went into the bathroom and sat down on the toilet, ready to look through the newspapers.

141

II

The Greek prime minister, Alexis Tsipras, declines once again to pay back his country's enormous loan from the International Monetary Fund and calls the final offer of his European creditors "unrealistic." . . . *The United States seeks an agreement that will keep Iran from obtaining nuclear arms for at least a decade; its diplomatic negotiators will be in Paris this week to discuss the topic of the Islamic State* . . . *A hotel has been located where ISIS houses virgins and other women to satisfy their militia* . . . *In Turkey, three US-made F-16s with Moroccan flags have disappeared. "I hope to see my son alive," one of the pilots' fathers tells the press; he is a schoolmaster in Rabat* . . . *In Qatar a storehouse has been found with archaeological objects taken by ISIS in Palmyra* . . . *A powerful movement, with a new and bloody caliphate, reaching across almost an entire continent, from Morocco to Pakistan, has today entered its terminal phase,* wrote a columnist.

He let the shower stream over his head and back, trying to clear his mind. Possibly the boy was following him. Would he be lying in wait for him at the hotel entrance? Should he call Singer to ask him about this? After all, wasn't it possible that *someone else* was watching him—not on the American's orders but on those of some other person or group equally interested in Abdelkrim's memory card?

He got out of the shower, dried himself off, and quickly got dressed. He turned on his laptop (it was almost ten already) and connected to the internet. He bought a plane ticket for that afternoon to Paris and requested his boarding pass. He had to be at the airport by three o'clock. He decided to leave his room at the Atlas just as it was; he would take with him only a change of clothes and the laptop, which fit in his Moroccan basket. He peeked out the bathroom window, which looked onto a narrow and shady back courtyard, where the hotel maids hung the sheets and towels to dry. He saw a metal door that opened onto the street; he'd be able to slip out that way. But he was on the fifth floor.

He picked up the basket and left the room. He went down the service stairs without running into anyone and reached the second floor. At the end of a hallway, he saw a service cart. The doors of several rooms were open wide, and he could hear the voices of two or three women. Walking lightly, he hurried a few meters and went into the first room, almost identical to his own. He closed the door softly and locked it. He sighed with relief and waited a moment to be sure no one was walking down the hallway. He went into the bathroom, to the window that looked down on the laundry courtyard. He managed without difficulty to climb through and lower himself to the ground. His heart beating madly, he saw the courtyard door was open, and he crossed through it. A dark hallway led to a workers' entrance, its door locked only from the inside. *Hamdul-lah.* Moving quickly, but without breaking into a run, he soon left the hotel behind, his suitcase still unpacked.

On Calle de Fez, he decided to cross through the small market to get to Calle de Holanda. As always, the odors of roses and fresh meat wafted through the aisles near the entrance. Once inside the market, he stopped in front of a stall selling dried fruits.

"Nus kilo," he told the vendor, pointing to a hill of stacked dates on a blue plastic basin. He looked down the aisle, then up. Nobody was following him.

"Shjral?"

"Tlatin dirham."

He counted out thirty dirhams.

"B'saha," the man said to him. "Enjoy."

He took a walk around the lower part of the market, crossed to where the spices were sold. Looking over his shoulder one more time, he came out onto Calle de Holanda.

In his room at the Villa de France, he opened the little packet of dates, ate three or four, and set the pits on the sill of

Matisse's famous window. *Still life on windowsill,* he thought, the date pits in the foreground.

He took Carrie's computer out of the pillowcase, opened it, and turned it on. *I ought to erase Abdelkrim's files,* he thought. He dragged them to the recycle bin, then tried to empty it, but a box opened on the screen saying, "Error! Bad code."

He tried again—one, two, three times. The error persisted. He scratched his head. *It can't be,* he thought.

It was ten to eleven when he phoned Boujeloud. He was on his way, he said.

"I'll wait for you in the parking lot."

"Ouakha, khay."

He called Singer. No answer. He left a voicemail; he would be a little late, he apologized.

At eleven o'clock sharp, he met Boujeloud in front of the hotel. He didn't want to tell him he was leaving that same afternoon or that he was afraid he was being followed. (He would regret this immediately.)

"Tell Carrie I'm very grateful."

"B'slemah, my friend."

"B'slemah."

He went back to the Matisse room. He looked one more time at the landscape out the window. He left the date pits where they were.

Suddenly it was as if someone had seized him by the throat. The boy in the yellow shirt that Sultán had pointed out

146

was standing in front of the gardens of Saint Andrew. On Calle de Inglaterra he saw Boujeloud's Mercedes pulling out, just as another Mercedes, black, came rapidly up Calle de América del Sur and crossed in front of Boujeloud's, forcing him to slam on the brakes. Boujeloud's arm gestured out the car window. He stuck his head out, upbraiding the other driver. A man dressed in black quickly approached from behind his car and struck him in the temple with his fist; Boujeloud's head and arm disappeared into the car. The man who'd hit him looked around; he had a beard and dark glasses.

Shit, the Mexican thought as he drew back. Had he been seen?

The bearded man put his hand through the car window, opened the door, and climbed into the car. The other Mercedes now left the street open. Boujeloud's Mercedes, with a squealing of tires, traced a semicircle and disappeared—toward Bou Araquía? The boy in the yellow shirt had also disappeared.

"Shit," he said, thinking of Boujeloud.

The phone began to ring. It was Singer.

"Hello?"

"I just got your message. Where are you?"

"David, something has just happened that I can't understand. Something terrible. I think a friend of mine has just been kidnapped. Have you had somebody watching me? Somebody following me?"

"What? Why would you say that? What happened?"

"Forget it," he said. "It could be my paranoia."

"What are you talking about? Do you want me to come get you? Where are you?"

The Tangier landscape he had seen in the Matisse window was changing into something else. He heard Singer's voice continuing to ask questions. Disoriented, he hung up. He didn't trust Singer, even though he wasn't certain of his involvement with what had just happened. It was possible someone else had learned about Abdelkrim's memory card. It was possible he was involved in a "very delicate" matter, as Singer had suspected.

A long flight of stairs plunged directly across the gardens of the Grand Hotel Villa de France, ending at a gate of iron lances that opened onto the triangle of streets where the brief and violent scene had occurred. The Mexican descended the stairs with the basket containing his change of clothes, his laptop, and his djellaba, his cell phone pressed to his ear. He was trying to reach Carrie, but she was not picking up.

III

A chain and a lock stopped him. He slung the basket over his shoulder and started to scale the gate.

"*Shni bgrit?*" he heard behind him.

He turned his head. It was an old gardener, whom he didn't know.

"You can't do that, *sidi*."

The Mexican couldn't get his leg over the sharp lances.

"Come down from there, *sidi*."

He obeyed. The gardener held the basket so that he could get down.

"*Smaheli.* Excuse me," the Mexican said. "I've got to get out . . ."

"*Blati.*"

He took a large rusty key out of his pocket to open the lock.

The gate opened with a squeak.

"*Shukran b'sef!*"

"La shukran. Al-lah wa shib."

He headed down Calle de Inglaterra to the Zoco de Fuera, where there were two lines of taxis. He got into a small one and asked the driver to take him to Souani.

IV

The Souani garden was under construction. The lawn had been taken out, and a mini bulldozer was digging a trench that ran toward the center of the roundabout. Small groups of uniformed students sat on the cement benches, and an ice cream vendor pushed his musical cart along the circular sidewalk. In the shade of a flowering date palm, a workman assembled a small chainsaw. A curtain of dry vines covered the upper part of the trunk, some twenty meters high. *They're going to cut it down,* he thought unhappily. And then, as if scandalized by his own triviality, *They've kidnapped my friend, and I'm thinking of this!* The café Al-Achab, where Mohammed used to meet his friends, was silent. Several Moroccans sat at tables all along the wall. Some were smoking. Two played cards in a corner. He sat down at a table on the terrace and ordered coffee. He tried to reassure himself again that he was not being followed. He paid for the coffee—the chainsaw had begun to buzz—and crossed the roundabout. On a little uphill street, he walked into the small labyrinth of the Souani medina. He got lost immediately. He turned around in a dead-end alley, inquired in a *baqal*, and in the end found Number Eleven. He wanted to make sure, for the last time, that no one had followed him. The street, very narrow, was deserted. Two cats fought over a fish skeleton just in front of Mohammed's door. The smell of decomposition was strong. He rang the bell. Rahma opened and let him in.

"Mohammed is upstairs," she said. "With Abdelkrim."

"Ah," he said, only slightly surprised. Somehow he had expected to find him here.

Mohammed was seated on a *m'tarba* under one of his paintings, an abstraction of eyes and noses. Barefoot, he leaned against the wall, silent and apparently very tired. Abdelkrim, thin and tall, stood in front of him. Another boy, younger than Abdelkrim and still beardless, stood at his side.

"Salaam aleikum."

"Aleikum salaam."

They invited him to sit. The youngest, who barely looked at him, left the room to prepare tea. He wore a green shirt. But he had the awkward demeanor of the boy Sultán had pointed out in the street.

"Do you recognize Abdelkrim?" asked Mohammed.

"Of course." He looked like Mohammed, but twenty or so years younger, with almond-shaped eyes like Rahma's.

"You came here once for a party my father threw for Mr. John. It was his birthday."

That couldn't be right, he thought, but decided not to contradict him.

"Yes," Abdelkrim said. "I remember you clearly. Or perhaps you have a double?"

This was the child prodigy.

"It's an honor to know you," he told him. "The first Moroccan astronaut!"

Mohammed, his face tense with worry, looked at the Mexican. He shook his head.

"They didn't grant him US citizenship. He cannot be an astronaut."

"How's that?"

"He's too Muslim, they told him."

"What? That's terrible. Very bad. So . . . ?"

"So nothing. Screw them."

Abdelkrim said, "My father gave you some tapes and a memory card—do you have them with you?"

He nodded yes, pointing to the basket, which he'd left next to the stairwell.

"The tapes are there. The memory card here." He touched his front pants pocket.

"All right. The tapes—have you listened to them?"

"Of course."

"And the memory card?"

He took it out of his pocket.

"Here it is," he said, and handed it over.

"All right," Abdelkrim said again.

"I could only decipher the first ones."

"Ah?"

Abdelkrim looked at his father.

"A friend helped me with the parts in Darija."

"A friend? What friend?"

He explained who Boujeloud was.

"Ah," said Mohammed, "that *djibli*."

He was about to tell them what had happened to Boujeloud. Instead he began to explain that he hadn't been able to read the card on his PC; he talked about his visit to the legation. They listened without interruption.

"Singer read only the first letters," he assured them. "Did you write them? He seemed impressed. Do you know the imams?"

"What computer did you use?" Abdelkrim wanted to know.

"A friend of mine's—her name is Carrie. She lent it to me."

Mohammed made a grimace of disgust.

"Singer used a PC?" Abdelkrim asked. "He put the card in a PC?"

"I think so. Yes, he put it in."

"All right," Abdelkrim said again.

Mohammed shook his head and turned to the Mexican.

"The legation is full of informers. I thought you knew that. It has always been full of informers. You cannot trust anyone. No one—I mean no one, my friend."

He agreed. He didn't know whom to trust anymore. He said he feared someone was watching him, and decided to tell them what had happened with Boujeloud.

Mohammed spoke to Abdelkrim in Darija: "And you can't trust this one either."

Abdelkrim looked at him.

"Can you tell me who was following you?"

"Same age, same build as Slimane here. Yellow shirt."

Rahma appeared on the staircase. Without coming up to the level of the living room, visible only from the waist up, she said something in Darija to Mohammed that the Mexican didn't understand.

"Can you have lunch with us?" Mohammed asked him.

He explained he had to be in Ibn Battouta at three to catch a plane to Paris.

"Slimane will take you. No problem."

V

Abdelkrim went into the room that Mohammed used as a studio; its only window looked out on the street. He closed the door, and the room darkened. Mohammed and the Mexican could hear the sound of a computer turning on. Slimane served a second round of tea.

"Friend," said Mohammed after a prolonged silence (although he managed to hear Abdelkrim talking on the phone behind the door in a language he couldn't understand), "wouldn't you like to have a smoke?"

"Why not?" he answered without thinking. It was a mistake. He didn't need anything to feed his paranoia.

Mohammed set to preparing the pipe, an old sebsi that he hadn't used for years. He asked Slimane to reach for his *motui*.

"A friend brought me this kif a few days ago," Mohammed explained while he opened the skin wrapping that held the kif. "It had been a long time since I'd seen him, and he didn't know I'd stopped smoking. *Hamdul-lah*. It smells very good. Try it."

He took the pipe, and Mohammed, ceremonious now, put a match to it. He drew on the pipe, held the smoke in his lungs for a moment, exhaled from his mouth, and then from his nose. The kif was excellent.

"M'sien b'sef."

Abdelkrim came back to the small room, sat beside him, and said in a low voice, "I think someone is following you, friend. Someone followed you here."

"But how?"

"I don't know. But they are circling the house, and I think it is because of you."

"I took every precaution," he said.

Abdelkrim was looking at the basket that still sat next to the stairwell.

"Can I see what you have in there? You don't mind?"

He examined every single object. He put the cassettes aside. ("These," he said, addressing no one, "I'd better keep.")

He opened the Mexican's laptop.

"May I?"

The Mexican nodded.

Abdelkrim put a cushion on his knees for the laptop. He looked through the main menu, clicked on two or three files (recent items), and turned it off. He seemed satisfied.

"I don't understand. What's going on?" the Mexican said.

"Your telephone—can I see it?" Abdelkrim asked.

He took it out of his pocket and handed it to him.

Abdelkrim examined the phone carefully—the front, the sides, the back. He turned it off, took off the cover, extracted the battery, the SIM card. He put it back together and handed it to the Mexican.

"It's better if you don't use it now, if you don't want them to monitor you. Your phone is completely open," he explained. "Anyone can hack into it. Anyone can follow your calls and know who you're with and what you're talking about."

"OK," the Mexican said.

Abdelkrim closed his eyes, leaned his head back, and opened his eyes again. He said, "What are we going to do?"

Slimane had his eyes fixed on the floor next to the Mexican's feet.

"This guy deserves what's coming to him," he said in Darija.

The Mexican acted as though he hadn't understood.

"Abdelkrim, I don't get it," he said. "Why would they follow me?"

Abdelkrim didn't answer.

"For the tapes, for the memory card?" the Mexican continued.

"The truth is my father was wrong to give them to you," Abdelkrim said. "I have many enemies."

VI

All causes are valid, he thought. *Men turn them good or bad.*

In Darija, Abdelkrim said to Slimane, "Go into the room and pray."

Then he looked at Mohammed. "Father, go down and eat with Rahma. Don't wait for us. We'll be down in a minute."

The boy and the man both obeyed him. When they were alone, Abdelkrim got up from his *m'tarba*, went over to the chest of drawers, and picked up a television remote. He turned on a monitor mounted in a corner of the ceiling; the Mexican hadn't noticed it before. He pushed some buttons, and the Mexican stared at the screen.

"It was no mistake, friend. Everything is planned," Abdelkrim told him. "Look closely. You won't see images like this again. Perhaps never. I hope never."

Two bearded men, their faces covered, were speaking in Arabic—were they Syrian? They looked at the camera. A woman's voice translated from Arabic to French, while two lines of subtitles crawled at the bottom of the screen, one in Arabic, the other in English. The image changed to a shot taken in Somalia: two US soldiers were raping a Somalian girl. It switched again, to a scene of tortures in Abu Ghraib, then another in Guantanamo. Then—and this terrified the Mexican most of all—the screen showed a Central American jail ("Juvenile Reformatory, Las Gaviotas, Guatemala," said the title), where some rioting prisoners were conducting a human sacrifice. While they jumped up and down to the beat of a Satanic band, they cracked open a man's chest on some concrete steps they'd converted into an altar, and pulled out his heart. As Abdelkrim narrated, the images changed from one horror—a Kurdish girl testifying to the series of rapes she had endured (all in the name of God)—to another: on a Mediterranean beach, a young Englishman cut the throat of a young Australian (blond, blue eyed) accused of betraying the cause of the Prophet.

All mafias—the gangs, the cartels, the governments; the Vatican, the patriarchs, and the ulema—all were as good as they were bad.

The Mexican had stopped listening. He was transfixed by the images, his hands soaked in sweat.

"Yes," Abdelkrim was saying. "We've had to become double agents . . . But you aren't listening?"

He regretted having smoked the kif.

"What was that?"

"These operations were necessary so that certain matters could be understood. You're a writer. Maybe you can understand this."

He reached out his hand and touched the Mexican's thigh. The touch paralyzed him. He nodded his head, and the other man withdrew his hand. He had laid the memory card there. The Mexican put it back in his pocket.

"Sorry, but we had to be very careful." Now Abdelkrim was smiling. He turned off the TV. "Now we know we can trust you."

"It's no problem," he said, relieved. "Go ahead."

"We need someone to write our story, even if we fail. *Especially* if we fail. Would you like to be part of our network?"

"Me?" he said, but it was less a question than an exclamation, almost a protest.

"We work for the Americans, it's true. At times we've had to work against them. And also for the European Space Agency. Today we may seem complicit with ISIS, or with AQMI. For us, everyone is right, and everyone is wrong. The kings, the presidents, those who believe in the vote, those who do not . . ."

"What do you call yourselves, your organization?"

"We don't have a name. We don't want to have one."

"Who backs you?"

Abdelkrim smiled. That he could not reveal. They received donations, but they were anonymous, he said. "And voluntary."

"Are you anarchists?"

"Anti-arms more than anything else. The state, the states, are our common enemy. Of course, so is ignorance. But these days all of us, or almost all of us, are deeply ignorant."

The Mexican was confused. He moved his head doubtfully.

"Do you know the story of the Yazidi people?" Abdelkrim continued. "Their Muslim neighbors call them devil worshippers. Right. They deny it. The word *devil* or *Satan* in fact doesn't exist, has never existed, in their language. They don't use symbols, they don't have a holy book or prophets. That's all. That wouldn't seem to justify the Muslims' wish to exterminate them, would it? We don't think so. They believe that even Iblis, the Muslim devil, whose name should never be uttered, has already been (or will be, since, for Allah, time does not exist) forgiven. Your God is omnipotent too, no? Why can't he pardon the devil, then? We can see and understand the perspectives of hatred and of love, of sin and virtue, which are man's creations. They are ours. We can see, so to speak, good and evil from the inside and from the outside. If we try."

"I'm stupefied," the Mexican confessed.

"Ha, ha, ha, ha, ha! My friend, that means you have understood something."

"I think so," said the Mexican. "But I'm not . . . I can't be sure."

"Without knowing it, you have already helped us—by listening to those tapes, by trying to decipher those memory cards. We have infected our enemies, who surround us. Your plane leaves at five? Let's go. There's not much time. I'll explain," Abdelkrim told him.

They went down to the dining room together.

VII

During lunch, Abdelkrim explained how he and his network had rescued virgins in Syria and how, in order to do so, some of his group had worked with—had had to work with—ISIS. On the other hand, members of his organization had acted as intermediaries in the multimillion-dollar sale of a series of eighth-century Manichaean manuscripts, but again, to do so, they had had to help enrich and empower an Israeli extremist group. There are many such examples, Abdelkrim assured him. Exploited orphans here, rape victims there, victims of diseases not yet known, even endangered species, and "a very long et cetera," he said as they ate their lunch.

"And why not have a name?" he wanted to know.

"We're not politicians" was the Moroccan's answer.

Rahma's voice came from the kitchen, incomprehensible to him.

Abdelkrim asked for tea.

"Just a moment," the Mexican said. "What will become of Boujeloud? Do you know?"

"Your musician friend? Don't worry."

"But I do worry."

Abdelkrim closed and opened his eyes. "You have my word," he said. "He'll be fine. When the time comes, I will give you proof."

"Who was it that took him?"

"AQMI."

"The Maghrebi Al-Qaeda?"

"Yes, we have friends there as well, *khay*."

VIII

They went back up to the living room.

Abdelkrim clapped his hands twice loudly and called, "Slimane!"

Slimane came out of Mohammed's study, looking pale. *Caught jerking off*, the Mexican thought.

The boy said, "*Khay*, we're surrounded."

Abdelkrim told the Mexican, "Don't worry. It's not yet time." He looked at his watch. It was after two.

He thought, *I'm going to miss my plane.*

As if he'd read the Mexican's thoughts, Abdelkrim said, "Don't worry. If we can count on strength enough to change the world, we should be able to delay a plane."

"I don't know," he said.

Without saying more, Abdelkrim walked down the stairs. He didn't stop in the dining room, however, but continued to the main floor. Slimane went back into the studio, and the

Mexican sat down on a *m'tarba*. Habit was stronger than reason, and he prepared another pipe of kif.

Abdelkrim came back a few minutes later and said, quietly, enigmatically, "The death of someone in this house will save you."

Then he cried, "Slimane!" and in Darija, "Go downstairs and talk with my father."

Slimane came out of the studio and went downstairs to join Mohammed.

Some of Rahma's relatives lived on the ground floor of the Zhrouni house; they were of *djebala* origin, Abdelkrim began to explain.

"Just a few minutes ago," he said in a very low voice, "the oldest daughter—she was fifteen—took her own life. They dishonored her yesterday. Today she hanged herself, the poor girl. She will be hanging in hellfire." He stopped. "But her death has saved you."

According to Moroccan custom, when someone dies, the burial has to take place the same day, and before sunset. The news of the girl's death had spread rapidly, and the little streets around Number Eleven were filling up with people.

The body would be taken to the Souani mosque, where men would pray for the girl, while family members, female friends, and other women of the neighborhood would wait. Then the procession would go on foot to the Al Moujahidine cemetery, a little more than a kilometer from Souani. Abdelkrim went downstairs again, where the Mexican could hear him talking with Rahma and Mohammed. It seemed to him they were saying they should wait.

At about three (*I've missed my flight,* the Mexican was saying to himself), a din rose up from the street. The Mexican went into the studio and looked out the window.

A large crowd, almost entirely women, had gathered—dangerously, he thought—in the little descending street, which seemed as if it couldn't hold any more people. Dizziness, an irrepressible fear was overtaking him. This wasn't the kif—it couldn't be the kif—he said to himself, aware now that he was passing out. His head hit the thickly carpeted floor of Mohammed's studio. *Hamdul-lah!*—he heard a voice say deep inside.

A few minutes later, the men walked out of Mohammed's house carrying two bodies, indistinguishable from each other, wrapped in a single shroud. They made their way down to the street among waves of wailing. And the procession started off, at a quickening pace, to the sound of cries and clapping.

Joyride

I

When he came to, he was standing in the middle of a crowded street that curved gradually between five- and six-story buildings, descending almost unnoticeably. The shop signs, competing for the visible space, were written in both Arabic and Latin letters. They were all incomprehensible.

He walked along slowly, bewildered, like someone who has had too much to drink, but he didn't remember having drunk anything at all. He stopped at a corner, looking for a street name. *"Istiklal,"* read some golden letters on a ceramic plaque. *Istiqlal* meant independence, he remembered. Why a *k* instead of a *q*? Wasn't this Avenida Al Istiqlal, then, in Tangier?

Without thinking, present and past confusing themselves in his mind, he put his right hand into his pants pocket. The pants, made of thick linen, were baggy, and the pocket was deep, widening toward the bottom. With two fingers, he took out a piece of paper, which was folded twice and covered with small, tight handwriting, a handwriting resistant to cursive—a woman's hand? *"Take funicular to Karaköy. Ferry to Üsküdar. Enter Şemsi Ahmet Pasha mosque. Approach camera. Sirkeci train station at three."* From the other pocket, he took out a weathered fifty-lira bill. It was Turkish. He was in Istanbul!

He felt a shudder run through his body, then a powerful dizziness. Down the street, the darkness of a passageway that led farther to the right caught his eye, and he set off in a straight line toward the shade. He walked down marble stairs whose center had been warped by generations of human steps. He sat down in a Turkish coffee shop with a very narrow terrace; a waiter soon came to take his order. The waiter smiled from under a thick mustache; his good humor seemed irrepressible.

"Coffee," the Mexican asked.

"Turkish?"

"Yes, Turkish, please."

With the fine powder of the coffee on his palate, a memory suddenly crystallized in some bypath of his brain—or was it not a memory?

He saw himself wrapped from head to toe in large, damp towels—or was the membrane enveloping him made of something else entirely?—and stretched out on his back on a slab of hot marble. His eyes were open. He looked up at an enormous cupola with holes in the shape of stars and circles and, beyond the cupola, the evening sky. Was it a hexagonal mausoleum? Firm, expert hands washed his body. He felt voluptuously transported back in time. The hands working on him reduced him to a fetal position—he was a baby being bathed for the first time. Tepid water trickled over his head, his shoulders, his back. The hands stretched him out face up on the marble. And now he felt that he was an old man, that this was the future, that he was already dead. This was his final ablution. Yet, without a doubt, this was a memory! Even now, he felt as if those respectful, reverent hands were washing him for the last time.

He lowered his eyes to the palm of his hand. A Turkish coin. Symbols, strange words. The cipher: 3.50. Now hands and bodies were pushing him forward. He saw himself compelled to pass through a revolving steel door (*a valve,* he thought) that would not let him move backward again.

He stood on the prow of a modern ferry, hemispheric like an outdated version of a flying saucer. It swayed softly over the liquid sapphire of the Bosphoros—or were they on the Golden Horn? A woman in a black caftan, her hair held by a salmon-colored scarf, her eyes hidden behind mirrored sunglasses, walked hurriedly to his right, giving him a small push, and uttered something harsh that he couldn't understand. A Turkish insult? It was three forty-five, as he could see on the huge wristwatch of a tall, obese man to his left who was talking on his phone. Out of the flesh of this man's hand—its wrist sporting a black Weekender—two or three of his own could have been fashioned.

A fresh breeze came up from the south, and the crests on the small waves began to multiply.

"Üsküdar, Üsküdar," he kept hearing around him. A group of giddy tourists was boarding the ferry then and gathered a few steps away from him at the guardrail, laughing. Amid the landscape of minarets, pointed sharply like pencils, and bulky cupolas, the golden spire of a Romanesque tower shone in the yellow afternoon sun. Several bloodred flags flew over the houses and the hills, over the trees in the park, and over the water. Seagulls came and went, crying out desperately at the blue wind.

"Where are you going?"

A young Turk, smiling excessively, was resting on the rail between him and the tourists.

"To the mosque."

"The Sinan mosque?"

He nodded.

"Argentinian?"

He didn't feel like replying.

"Don't you want some company?"

"No, thanks."

The young man, irritated, pushed away from the guardrail and went into the ferry cafeteria, where the darkness swallowed him up. The ferry moved quickly over the water. The huge European cruise ships, anchored at the edges of the channel—*Queen Victoria*, *Norwegian Spirit*—soon fell behind them. The houses of the Pera district, beyond the boats, yawned in the afternoon glare.

It was a chaotic world, and he stood at the center of the chaos. *Here, now,* he thought, the wind whipping around his head and the water splitting beneath the double keel of the Turkish ferry. Red flags waved everywhere.

The ferry veered and slowed down. The smallest of the mosques of Sinan faced him from the other side of the street, beyond the docks—a majestic, pale-gray cupola. When the ferry touched the shore, four or five seagulls hovered in the air over the heads of the passengers. A crow flew among the seagulls, scattering them, and traced a straight line toward the mosque. Behind the ferry, and very near, an empty cargo ship—the waterline was much too high, he thought—blasted its powerful horn. He could read on the hull, far above his head, the name *Asir*, underneath an Egyptian eye. He felt a faint vertigo. Everything seemed insane. Arabic characters, written in gold in a long turquoise panel outside the mosque shone like jewels from across the street. He was standing now on the Asian shore.

He knelt, barefoot, under the mosque's splendid cupola, in imitation of the prostrate Muslims in front of a mihrab. Four or five times, his forehead touched the red carpet of the faithful. A waft of cool air from an air conditioner surprised him. Near the entrance was a panel with numerous surveillance monitors. He raised his face to one of the cameras, which seemed to cover every corner of the mosque. No one came up to him. No one even glanced at him.

On the return trip, in Sirkeci, he went into the waiting room of the old train station, where several men with thick beards and shaved heads were rehearsing a performance of whirling dervishes. Near a newspaper kiosk, a small man gave him a brochure with information on the next *semas*. On the back of the brochure, he read, written in crude letters with a yellow Magic Marker, in English, *"Back to Pera by tunnel. Drink at Pera Palace."*

This part of the city, with its steep, narrow streets, reminded him of San Francisco. He was now on the street called Istiklal. It didn't take him long to find the Pera Palace Hotel.

On the terrace, which seemed deserted, he sat down at one of the central tables, looking eastward, where the massive Marmara hotel blocked the view of the sky. In one of the French windows of the ninth or tenth floor, a man—tall, slender, in a gray suit—consulted his watch while he talked on the phone. He looked down at the terrace, then abruptly stepped back out of view. That seemed perfectly natural. On the back of his bar receipt, the Mexican read. *"Özkaya museum at 7."*

II

At the end of the road that led to the stately museum on top of the hill, a woman stood, dressed in white, her shoulders and arms bare. She did not seem to be—she could not have been—the hostess. But was she waiting for him? Tall, svelte, her chestnut hair falling over her shoulders, she brought to mind one of the caryatids of the Erechtheion. And she *was* waiting for him, because when he came within two or three steps of her, she held out her hand. Her eyes, gray and luminous, overcame him.

"You're right on time. Very good. There are some people you must meet."

Her voice seemed familiar. Did he know her? The woman walked as if she were in a hurry. He followed her along a white gravel path, over a spongy lawn, and to a very wide terrace, where people were celebrating. A band was playing Italian music. The female singer went very well with the scenery: a set for a spy movie.

Everything, he thought (or remembered?) had been arranged.

He felt he was complicit in it all, and yet he was also irrationally happy. For the first time, as she stopped beside a small group of people and whispered into his ear, "Let me introduce you," he inhaled the woman's scent.

His mouth closed, and he couldn't find anything to say. He nodded.

His last name was not Rubirosa; it was a misunderstanding. He was about to clarify this, but the woman shot him a glance, and he kept quiet.

An older man, a head taller than he, said, "A writer?" He gripped his hand and added, "We've been needing one!" His voice, smooth and silky, seemed nevertheless frank. "Thank you, Nada, for bringing him!"

Nada. Was it a nom de guerre, like Rubirosa?

"Xeno recommended him, and I was lucky enough to find him," she said. He swelled a little with happiness to hear the note of pride in her voice and to know he was the cause of it. He laughed, belatedly. He gave his hand to a Greek princess and a French collector, and then Nada took him by the arm and drew him out of the little circle to resume what seemed to be her mission.

"Some of them have read about you," she whispered again, and again her perfume distanced him from what he was hearing and seeing. Her low voice ("I put you up online; I wrote a

Wikipedia article and everything. I'm sure some of these people have googled you."), the music (an Italian song about the world turning and turning in infinite space), the procession of elegant citizens with their luxury and their jewels—this was all scenery. The essence of the drama was this woman. Other rounds of introductions continued on the terrace: a scientist and a collector of Byzantine art; an Indian astronomer; the heir to a famous Austrian fortune; an English duke; an Egyptian magnate turned philanthropist during the Syrian refugee crisis; a US billionaire; another Mexican—they were all there.

Now the musicians were playing an old French tango.

The woman's thick, well-defined eyebrows arched on her luminous forehead, and her nose, which was too large, elevated her to a point beyond beauty. She stopped, facing an arch set upon Doric columns: the entrance to another gallery of the vast museum. He read, "SEA: Swords into Ploughshares; Missiles into Satellites."

"SEA?" he asked.

"Space-era art," she explained. "Let's go in."

What did it matter who she really was or what her name was or where she came from? He walked two or three paces behind her, in the wake of her delicate odor, which was either intoxicating him or doing something very much like it. He had heard of scents that contained some drug or pheromone. Hers had to be one of those. What did it matter? He marched on, happily, from one place to the next, beside this perfect woman, who showed him off proudly to the world. What more could he want? He wanted her. Perhaps it wouldn't last, he reflected. Did it matter? No! But he would make it last as long as it could. To the extent of his modest possibilities, he would make it everlasting. He took a glass of red wine from a young waitress with the bearing of a film actress, resolving to drink it very slowly.

III

"This gentleman is Pontekorvo," she said. "Nick. An old friend. One of my best friends."

"Rubirosa? The writer?"

A triangle of knowing looks.

"Sometimes," he said, and Pontekorvo laughed. Did he know everything? Probably.

"Brilliant," said Pontekorvo in a serious voice, and looked around him. "Brilliant."

He didn't know what to say.

She: "Everybody's here." But now she appeared rather worried.

"Xeno wants to talk to you," the Greek adventurer said, and looked toward the threshold of a door behind him to the right. "Just through there."

"Xeno? All right."

She took him by the hand. "Shall we?"

He agreed once again, wrapped in the sphere of perfumed light that seemed to emanate from the woman or from her long white dress, which she held up with both hands to go up or down the stairs, showing her ankles. He went on walking behind her. (A line descended from between her shoulders to her waist and oscillated with her walking.) They stepped over the threshold and took a wide curved staircase down into a much grander hall than the one they'd been in. Here was more food and drink, and a whole troop of waiters and waitresses that came and went among the people. An illuminated sign announced again, "SEA."

A woman in a blue-and-silver dress was the center of attention. A semicircle of guests gathered around to listen to her.

She whispered to him, "She's a goddaughter of the museum owner, and its director. I'll introduce you. But she doesn't like me. She's rich, extremely rich. Terrible taste."

The woman was taller and blonder than anyone else, and her arrogance was a general challenge.

He dared to say, "I don't want to know her, in that case."

She smiled. "No? She's an authority on ancient Iraqi art. In the museum basement, they have storerooms full of artworks. Mysteriously, or maybe not, the art keeps on coming. But let's go on. We have to find Xeno."

"Who's Xeno?" he asked.

They were in an empty salon with very high ceilings. One wall displayed contemporary artworks—abstract paintings fashioned from different kinds of metallic fibers and textiles.

"Expensive tapestry," she said. "Nothing more. And camouflage," she added in a very low voice.

In the middle of the room were sculptures made of wire and tubes of all sizes. Some suggested enormous convoluted honeycombs or nets of blood vessels; others, pipe organs or complex exhaust pipes. *The intestines of a giant,* he thought.

They passed through a rectangular room that featured an installation entitled *Negative Quarry*, reminiscent of the work of the Korean sculptor Lee Bul. There were hanging pieces, like enormous aluminum candelabra, chains of varying thicknesses, mirrors . . .

"Where did they get all this?" he asked.

He had paused to examine a vast, somewhat frayed golden cloth and, framed by the cloth, a series of ceramic tablets that could have been used to make a gigantic helmet.

"It matters less where it came from than where it's going," she joked enigmatically. And pointing to a tower of carbon fiber that reached to the ceiling, she added, "This is from a poet who thinks he's a sculptor."

He was particularly struck by a huge steel sphere, in which their two very reduced reflections appeared. (Since when did he have gray hair?) The sphere had a few dents here and there. It was called *The Moon*. On the other side of the moon, a black monolith suggested the realistic fantasies of Arthur C. Clarke. At the bottom, a little plaque read, "To the Unknown God"—as in the offerings of antiquity—"2016."

"What does Nick do?" it occurred to him to ask.

"Computer science. He was in charge of a lab at MIT. He knows everything, or almost everything, about cables, rockets, satellites. The slogan "Missiles into Satellites" isn't his, though. He plagiarized it from the author of *2001*, or at least that's what Nick says. He's a diver too. Do you know who Alan Bond is? He deciphered a clay tablet from Assyria, dating seven hundred years before Christ. It says that an asteroid that struck Earth caused huge floods in the Tyrol in 3123 BC. He connects this to the destruction of Sodom and Gomorrah. His last project is the Skylon, a new model of a spaceship that will make flights ten times cheaper than they are now."

"Did you see that film *Gravity*?"

She didn't deign to answer.

They had entered a hallway, a tunnel, at the end of which stood a large metal hatch. The hatch opened, and she stopped and invited him to go in.

"Will you wait for me here?" she asked.

"Where are you going?"

"I'll be back. You go ahead."

The hatch closed with an electric hum, and soon he was standing in complete darkness. When the light came back on, he was alone in a kind of vast planetarium. He saw above his head the firmament full of stars. He heard a voice reciting—and he recognized the cadence and the Buenos Aires accent—a fragment (albeit distorted) of "The Aleph."

The voice said, "I saw in a study of Alkmaar a globe of the world placed between two mirrors that multiplied it endlessly . . ."

The cupola of the planetarium had transformed itself into an astronomer's observatory. In the center of the hemisphere where he found himself, he saw a small rocket being lifted upright with steel cables. The whole thing began to seem like buffoonery. The outfit of the person coming toward him could not possibly be a space suit.

It was Abdelkrim who said, *"Salaam aleikum,"* from the other side of the glass, which reminded him of a diving mask. "Are you there?" he was about to ask. Instead he said, "I knew somehow that you would be here."

Behind Abdelkrim was Xeno.

The voice of Borges had stopped.

"That's the signal."

"What signal?"

"That after this there won't be any more signal. Look."

Xeno showed him the screen of his iPhone.

Nothing.

They invited him to get into the rocket, which now stood at a sixty-degree angle.

"Let's go."

He stopped. "And what happened to Boujeloud?" he suddenly wanted to know, with an abrupt recollection.

Abdelkrim's gloved hand squeezed his arm.

"He's all right. Let's go."

He wanted to resist. "Can you give me proof?"

"You have my word, my friend."

Xeno shook his head. "He had some bad luck," he said. "It wasn't our intention. AQMI let him go. But then the Americans got him—"

"It's all right. It was for Allah," the Moroccan cut him off.

Driss, Mohammed's other son, appeared on one side of the spaceship. He was dressed in immaculate white overalls and held a large monkey wrench in one hand.

"Are you afraid?"

Where is she? he wondered.

Looking at Xeno, the Mexican realized that he looked a lot like the woman. Xeno said,

IV

"Joyride?"

They can because they believe they can, he thought. He realized then that he was being used. "Why me?" he said very quietly.

She moved her head. But where had she come from?

"You seemed predestined," she told him. "Your stay in Morocco. And that article certainly helped. 'An Asian Fable.'"

"Predestined?"

"You don't see why?"

"Maybe," he said, not at all convinced. "But what if it hadn't worked?"

"That, my dear," she said, "is a futile question."

A siren began to sound, not very loud.

"We should hurry," she said. "Don't forget that they're looking for you."

"Looking for me?"

"You disappeared in Tangier."

"Who's looking for me?"

"A lot of people—Singer's friends, the bearded ones, your ex-wife, your goddaughter."

"Why?"

"They all have their reasons. To begin with, you infected, or helped to infect, the internet. In effect, the internet crashed, or began to—and it's still crashing—once you put Abdelkrim's memory card in those PCs."

"Are you serious?"

"Bad—very bad—code. Designed at MIT. That was brilliant," she said.

"How did I get here?"

"On a yacht, darling."

"From Tangier?"

She nodded and said, "Pity that you weren't able to see the scenery."

"You think it's funny?"

"It's a question of time," she said, "like almost everything. You'll be able to laugh too, in time."

"When did I get here?"

"Barely half a day ago."

But, he thought, he had gray hair; he didn't remember having gray hair in Tangier. *Canities subita?* Another kind of camouflage? Part of his new identity?

They were standing in front of the ship. On one side, diagonally, the name read, *"Osiris."*

"It was made to scale. With SABRE engines and everything. Can it fly? Supposedly it can take us up thirty-six thousand kilometers and even a little beyond that." She laughed—mischievously? "It's a compact Skylon, if you like. Sound familiar? An aluminum sculpture, some two hundred feet tall that they once put up on the shores of the Thames. But I was speaking of the ship, dear. Powell and Moya, the architects, would be very proud. Bond baptized his baby in honor of those men."

"Ridiculous," he said.

"Well, yes."

"This is art? We're in an art museum, aren't we?"

"As art per se, of course, I don't have any comment. But I think this is also something else. There's a message."

"What message?"

"Shall we board?"

They began to climb the aluminum ladder through a tunnel between the thrusters, the bowels of the ship.

"It's a game," she said.

"What's the object of the game?"

"Knocking out a few satellites," she explained. "Child's play."

They squeezed through a hatchway. The interior looked primitive. The control cables and the air hoses were exposed, and there was barely space for two reclining seats.

"Are we going to fly?"

"Well, of course."

"Who's the pilot?"

"An automatic pilot will do almost all the work. Abdelkrim will have to press a couple of buttons for liftoff and landing, nothing more."

"Didn't they kick him out of NASA?"

"Et bien voilà," she said.

V

"And the space suits?" he asked, half-serious, half-joking, before sitting down.

"We'll reach a final speed of ten kilometers per second. We'll leave the atmosphere and continue until we go beyond the orbit of almost all the satellites that we must . . . neutralize." She looked at her watch. "The trip will take between fifty and a hundred hours. What's that? We put on the suits down here. They're very heavy. Neither you nor I are trained for this, but don't worry. You can wear diapers. Here they are. Of course, you can strip; I'm not going to look. When we pass a hundred kilometers in altitude—just a few minutes after liftoff—you'll feel better. You'll weigh less. Shall I go on?"

It wasn't easy to get his pants off in that position—*the position of King Pacal of Palenque,* he thought, the Mayan cosmonaut—in a fully reclined seat, but he was managing.

"The truth is, there are no rules," she continued.

"Naturally," he managed to say.

"Satellites compete for space at high velocities; this is why the fastest, but also the dirtiest, way to bring them down is simply to send something into their path. The impact of an object as small as a marble can deactivate or destroy a satellite worth a billion dollars."

"Perfect!" he exclaimed.

"We could generate a chain reaction that would transform Earth's orbit into a demolition derby," she explained mechanically, while she finished fastening her suit.

He let out a first, tentative spurt of urine; he felt neither cold nor heat. He then released it all, with great pleasure.

"Once the satellites are neutralized," she said, "we will transmit our message. Nick and the rest of the team are taking care of the transoceanic cables and those of AT&T, GAFAM (Google, Apple, Facebook, Amazon, Microsoft), and their rivals, who constitute the biggest enemy in this regard. We pay for them to spy on us, right? Enemies on a payroll, like most servants. But that's another chapter. When we've completed the task, we'll return to the island of Leros to help the immigrants, who don't stop coming, in spite of the new laws. What do you think? Nobody will look for us there. We could also go to Qamishli, the secret capital of the Kurds in the Taurus Mountains, if you like. Or to Lalish, the sanctuary of the Yazidi, on the plains of Nineveh."

He didn't believe a word of it, but he said, "Sounds good to me."

"We could fail. We'll know soon enough."

They were sitting, shoulder to shoulder, in the little cabin of the built-to-scale spaceship, each looking at the starry sky through a separate porthole.

"Who am I running from?" he insisted.

She turned in her seat to look at him. She laughed.

"Well, who do you think you are?"

He thought, *I'm a prisoner.*

"Nothing," he said out loud. "Nobody."

He felt a tremor, but it was not the earth moving; it was the ship lifting off. He closed his eyes. He opened them. She was still there. Everything was all right.

On the terrace of the magnificent museum, everyone—from Asia, Europe, Africa, America, perhaps even from Oceania—fixed their eyes on an extraordinary event. The spaceship, no bigger than a small airplane, shooting up into the air, appeared to ignite, traced a furrow of flames, and then vanished into space, leaving behind a long, luminous tail. Everyone shouted. Exultant, Xeno turned to Nick, who was watching the sky with a flute of champagne in one hand, and embraced him joyously—as Aeneas had embraced Acestes, the lucky Mexican would write months later, at peace (without telephone, without internet), on Patmos, when the horrors and portents narrated here had already become, for the time being, things of the past.

EDITOR'S NOTE

The Skylon, an aluminum and steel sculpture in the form of a cigar, designed by Moya, Powell, and Samuely, was the symbol of the Festival of Britain in 1951. At a height of ninety meters, it was held in place by guy wires attached to the banks of the Thames in London's South Bank district. The following year, at Churchill's direction, it was sold as scrap and made into ashtrays.

ACKNOWLEDGMENTS

I owe the writing of this book to the hospitality of my friends: Claude Nathalie Thomas, Cherie Nutting, and Mohammed Mrabet in Tangier; Alexis Protonotarios on the island of Sifnos; Xenia Geroulanos in Patmos; and Ergin Iren in Istanbul. My thanks also to Magalí Rey Rosa, Alexandra Ortiz, Guillermo Escalón, and Horacio Castellanos Moya, who kindly read the manuscript; to Eduardo Rubio, the first Guatemalan astrophysicist, who enlightened me on orbital matters such as the Lagrangian Points; to my patient editors María Fasce and Lola Martínez de Albornoz, and to my agents Jessica Henderson and Cristóbal Pera for their advice and commentaries.

ABOUT THE AUTHOR

Rodrigo Rey Rosa was born in Guatemala in 1958. He immigrated to New York in 1980, and in 1982 he moved to Morocco. American expatriate writer Paul Bowles, with whom Rey Rosa had been corresponding, translated his first three books into English. Rey Rosa has based many of his writings and stories on legends and myths indigenous to Latin America and North Africa. Of his many works, seven have been translated into English: *The Beggar's Knife*, *Dust on Her Tongue*, *The Pelcari Project*, *The Good Cripple*, *The African Shore*, *Severina*, and now *Chaos, A Fable*. He currently lives in Guatemala City.

ABOUT THE TRANSLATOR

Photo © Christina Mojica

Jeffrey Gray, a professor at Seton Hall University in New Jersey, is the English translator of Rodrigo Rey Rosa's novels *The African Shore* (Yale University Press, 2014) and *Chaos, A Fable*. He is the author of *Mastery's End: Travel and Postwar American Poetry* (University of Georgia Press, 2005), as well as many articles on literature and American culture. His poetry has appeared in *American Poetry Review*, *Atlantic*, the *Literary Review*, *Mid-American Review*, *Notre Dame Review*, and other periodicals. He is a coeditor (with Ann Keniston) of *The News from Poems:*

Essays on the New American Poetry of Engagement (University of Michigan Press, 2016) and *The New American Poetry of Engagement: A 21st Century Anthology* (McFarland, 2013). He was born in Seattle, Washington, and has lived in Asia, the South Pacific, Europe, and Latin America.